KINGPIN WIFEYS
VOLUME 7

BY

K. ELLIOTT

Other Titles by K. Elliott

Kingpin Wifeys Series

Season I
Kingpin Wifeys Part 1
Kingpin Wifeys Part 2
Kingpin Wifeys Part 3
Kingpin Wifeys Part 4: Jada's Story
Kingpin Wifeys Part 5: Lani's Dilemma
Kingpin Wifeys Part 6: A Starr is Born
Kingpin Wifeys Part 7: Who Do You Love?
Kingpin Wifeys Part 8: Finale for Season 1

Season II
Kingpin Wifeys 1: A Dollar Before Sunset
Kingpin Wifeys 2: The Bad Guy
Kingpin Wifeys 3: Going Hard
Kingpin Wifeys 4: Black Widow
Kingpin Wifeys 5:If God is for Us
Kingpin Wifeys 6: Wages of Sin
Dilemma
Dear Summer
Entangled
Treasure Hunter
Street Fame

Godsend Series
Godsend 1: A Necessary Evil
Godsend 2: The Search for Rochelle
Godsend 3: Pissed All The Way Off
Godsend 4: Hiding In Plain Sight
Godsend 5: Blasphemy Out West
Godsend 6: All Jokes Aside
Godsend Full Length Novel: The Weight of Echo
Godsend 7: The Halo Effect
Godsend 8: The Value of a Woman
Godsend 9: Square In The Mouth
Godsend 10: That Stupid Hooker
Godsend 11: Taken for Granite
Godsend 12: The Audacity
Godsend 13: Selling Woof Tickets
Godsend 14: Ass to Kis

Chapter 1

BIRD SAT ON THE PASSENGER SIDE OF A RED Volkswagen; a forty-five-year-old Crip named Low Down drove. Low Down was a tall, thin, light-skinned man with droopy eyes. He drove slowly and carefully. From the rear view, Low Down noticed a silver Impala tailing them. He turned to Bird and said, "Hey, man, I think one-time is behind us." One-time was West Coast slang, referring to the police.

Bird didn't flinch. He never did when someone mentioned the police. The only time he did was when he was nine years old and he'd been riding with his father and another man. The friend to his father had warned that the police were behind them, and the nine-year-old Bird turned to see for himself. His dad slapped the fuck out of him and told him never to look back whenever someone said police. And to this day, Bird refuses to look back when police are following him.

"They may not be following us. Change lanes. You sound nervous."

"I am nervous," Low Down said. "Bruh, all this money and guns we got in here. Did you forget we just killed Avant?"

"Nobody knows this but us."

"Yeah, us and Black."

"Be cool, and if we get pulled I'll do the motherfuckin' talking."

Low Down held the wheel steady. "I know what the police looks like. I can see their badges."

A royal blue Ford Focus, two car lengths ahead, was in the far right lane. Low Down maneuvered past the Focus, and the police got behind them. A white Ford Explorer boxed them in from the left.

Sirens flashed and Low Down said, "We're fucked." He attempted to pull over in the median when the car had come to a complete stop.

Three white men and one black man with FBI jackets and guns drawn fenced them in. Bird reached for his Glock under the seat. An agent fired a shot and shattered the window. The bullet grazed Bird's temple.

"Hands up!"

Bird and Low Down complied. The officers yanked the men from the car and hurled their asses to the pavement.

Bird said, "What are you pulling us over for?"

The black man introduced himself. "I'm FBI Agent Daniels. Give me the money and we won't have an issue."

"What money?"

Daniels tapped his feet. "Now you're going to play with my intelligence?"

One of the agents removed the keys from the ignition and popped the trunk, spotted a briefcase, cracked it, and wads of cash spilled from it. A .380 and two AR15s were found under the spare tire.

Bird was still face-down on the pavement. Laughing but wanting to cry and his pride wouldn't let him. He said to Daniels, "You can't just do this; you have to have probable cause."

"You think so, huh?"

"You're going to need it when my lawyer finish with your ass."

A big white guy named Malarkey pressed Bird's head with a combat boot and said, "Say one more thing and I'll kick your goddamned teeth out."

Moments later, they loaded Bird and Low Down in the Ford Explorer as they searched the car.

Daniels found the rental car agreement from Hertz. A minute later, he plucked Bird and Low Down's wallets from their pockets. Bird's name was Brandon Hall; Low Down was Chance Washington of Long Beach, California. "What the hell are y'all doing out here?"

"Coming to Atlanta is not a crime last time I checked," Low Down said.

Kiyante Meeks's name was on the rental agreement. Daniels turned to an agent named Ray Teller and said, "Do an NCIC on these two, along with Kiyante Meeks." NCIC was an acronym for National Crime Information Center where national criminal history reports were gathered.

The officer ran the NCIC and returned seven minutes later. He said, "Got nothing on Meeks, but Hall and Washington got charges for days. Hall even had a kidnapping charge."

Daniels said, "Kidnapping? Damn."

"Look, I held my baby mama against her will and they called it kidnapping. You know how they do the black man." Bird said.

Daniels ignored his silly ass. "Meeks your girlfriend?"

"No."

Daniels said to Teller, "I bet you lunch at Chipotle he's lying, and she is his girlfriend."

Teller laughed and said, "You always know this kind of shit."

Chapter 2

WHEN THEY ARRIVED AT KIYANTE'S HOUSE SHE WAS exiting a silver G Wagon in her driveway. She noticed Daniels and Malarkey as she hopped out of the car, and stepped quickly toward the house.

Kiyante was a short woman with tiny breasts and an ample ass. Her face was oval and she had innocent eyes. She wore an olive mini skirt and six-inch Louboutins.

Daniels approached her and said, "Don't run. I just wanna talk."

She turned and faced him and asked "Talk about what?"

"I'm with the FBI."

"I can read." She stared at his jacket.

"We need to search your house."

"You said you wanted to talk." She rocked side to side. "Show me a warrant and you can search."

He presented the rental agreement to her.

"What is this supposed to mean?"

"This means I pulled your boyfriend over with guns and drugs in a car that you rented." Daniels was lying about the drugs, but Kiyante didn't need to know that right now. "Look, but there is no need for you to be afraid. This has nothing to do with you. Just let me search the house and I promise you will not go to jail."

The woman looked at Daniels for a long time. She started tapping her heels while contemplating.

"Kiyante, you have children?"

"Two boys."

"Bird ain't the father?"

"I thought you was the FBI?"

"I am."

"Well then you should know the answer to that question."

He smirked. She was feisty and she was kind of ghetto, but he liked it. He could never see himself with a woman like Kiyante, but he would definitely fuck her. "How old are the kids?"

"Seven and eight."

Daniels said, "My daughter is seven and my son is eight," he lied. He leaned in closely and said gently, "I'd hate for them to have to be brought up through the system."

"What do you mean?" She crossed her arms and huffed. "What do you want?"

"I don't want anything from you."

The next-door neighbors appeared, a middle-aged white couple walking a German Shepherd. They were staring in the direction of the conversation.

"Don't worry about them. I'll tell them that we are investigating a kidnapping. They won't know a thing."

"How long is it going to take to search the house?"

"It will be fast and we're not going to ransack the house."

"Where the fuck is Bird?" Kiyante asked.

Daniels glanced at his watch and said, "Right about now he should be downtown pacing in the drunk tank, wondering how in the hell he's going to get out the shit he's in."

She glanced at her watch. "I have somewhere to be."

Daniels nodded and stole a look her nipples, which were visible through her shirt. "I understand."

"You ain't got no warrant?"

"I can go get a warrant. Just wanted to see if you wanted to be cooperative. I don't want you to have to go down with Bird. Social Services is going to take your kids. I've seen it happen too many times." Daniels liked using kids as leverage to break women down. It worked time and time again.

"I don't—"

"Let's make a deal."

"I'm listening."

"Tell me where the drugs and money are stashed and I don't have to search your home."

She thought for a moment. Then she said, "Come inside."

Agent Malarkey waltzed over to the nosey-ass neighbors who were still standing at the edge of their yard, looking and playing with the dog at the same time.

The agent rubbed the German Shepherd's head and asked, "What's his name?"

"Jack," the old white man said. "Named after my father."

"He's beautiful."

"Thank you."

"You know, I knew they were trouble," the nosey-ass man said. "They have all kinds of expensive cars pulling up all times of night," he volunteered.

Malarkey ignored his ass then presented him with a picture of Ashanti Smith. "Have you seen her?"

"No."

"She went missing a few days ago. If you see her, call me." He handed them one of his business cards.

The couple nodded and said they would be on the lookout for her. They then disappeared inside.

Daniels followed Kiyante inside. He watched her disappear to the back and return with an army-green duffle bag.

"I have no idea what's in here."

"You don't?"

"No."

"Is there anything else I should know about?"

"Bird don't live here. He brought this over and asked me if I would keep it and I agreed."

Daniels nodded and said, "Thanks." He carried the bag out to the car and drove off with Malarkey.

• • •

It was eight in the evening and Bird and Low Down had now been bound in rope in the back of the Ford Explorer for many hours. Daniels cut their ropes and dropped them off on a long, winding dirt road in Forsyth, Georgia, a place that had been known for white supremacy. There was an old, dilapidated house just off the road, a big oak tree in front with a noose hanging from one of the limbs.

Daniels said, "Good luck, boys."

Bird said, "This is fucked up, man."

"If you run fast enough, you might make it out alive." He fired a shot in the air and skidded out of the area."

Bird said to Low Down, "We're fucked, bruh."

Chapter 3

FOR THE LAST THREE HOURS, DR. CRAIG MATTHEWS SAT on a stool in the middle of a cold interrogation room, picking boogers from his nose. Staring at them then flicking them clear across the room. He'd been picked up and charged with the murder of Anne Matthews, the mother of his children. Craig was also a suspect in an unrelated homicide.

Detective Kearns and Williams sat across from him. They were surprised when he said, "I want to make a deal."

"What kind of deal?"

"Take the death penalty off the table and I'll tell you everything that I know."

Kearns said, "Talk."

"I need some assurances, something in writing."

"We'll get you something in writing."

Craig smiled politely but not genuinely. He was defeated. His hair disheveled and nostrils damaged from years of drug abuse. He didn't want to be in jail but he was somewhat relieved that he could get some rest now.

"I wanna see my kids."

"You killed their mom."

"You don't know that. Let me see my kids."

"I'll see if I can make that happen," Williams said.

Detective Kearns stared at his phone, drooling over some Instagram fitness model doing squats.

Williams nudged him.

Kearns set the phone on the table and said, "That will be up to the D.A."

Craig dropped his head and said, "I need to be in protective custody."

"Why?"

Craig avoided eye contact. "I'll tell you everything you need to know."

"Think you're going to get hurt, good doctor?"

"More like afraid to get killed."

"I don't know if I can give you all of what you are asking for," Williams said.

Craig nervously tapped the table. "Either you do it or there is no deal."

"And you'll get the death penalty," Kearns said evenly.

"And spend money on a trial." Williams bit his bottom lip. "All I can do is try my best."

"Look, I need PC and I need to see my kids, Mr. Williams. Is that understood?"

Williams made way toward the door and Craig shouted, "Answer me, Mr. Williams!" Williams kept walking without responding.

"Answer me, Detective Williams!"

Williams exited the interrogation room.

●   ●   ●

Dressed in jeans, a dark blue North Face jacket, and matching Jordan's, Jada was about to make a quick dash to Lennox Mall when the doorbell rang. She opened the door for Starr.

"I need to talk."

They went into the kitchen. Jada poured herself a glass of white wine and offered Starr something before realizing that she was pregnant.

"What's on your mind?" Jada asked.

"I need your advice, but you cannot tell anybody my business."

"Of course not," Jada said. Then she thought about bitch-assed Fresh. She certainly wouldn't let him know anything that she and Starr would discuss. She knew that he would run and tell Q like he'd done before.

"Look, you know I'm pregnant."

"Yes."

"But I found out that the baby is not Q's."

"What?"

Starr dropped her head.

Jada gulped her wine down. Then poured more. "Whose baby is it? And how do you know it's not Q's?"

"The doctor told me that I was six weeks, I didn't sleep with Q then."

"Who is the baby's father?"

"Terrell."

"Who?"

"A basketball player. A client. I met him a few months ago. I decorated his home."

"Damn."

"I know, right." She avoided looking in Jada's direction. "Q is all excited."

"Damn, girl. So what are you going to do?"

"I don't know what to do."

"So just abort the baby and move on. Nobody has to know."

Starr looked very worried. "I can't."

"What do you mean you can't?"

"It just ain't right."

Jada sipped her wine then stood and paced, and this made Starr nervous.

"Jada, can you please sit down?"

Jada plopped back down in the chair and said, "I'm not understanding, baby girl. Why can't you just have an abortion and take this little secret to your death bed?"

"Terrell deserves to know."

"But you're going to have an abortion."

"I'm thinking of having one."

"If you have an abortion, why does he need to know?"

Starr began to cry and then said, "My conscience won't let me keep it from him."

Jada wanted to know where the fuck was this conscience when she was fucking two men during the same time period? But who was she to talk? Plus, the mistake had been made.

"Don't tell him."

"I have to."

"And what are you hoping to gain?"

"I just have to get it off my chest."

"I'll go with you."

"I can do it alone." Her lips trembled.

"What about Q?"

"I'm going to tell him that the baby is not his."

"What do you think he is going to say?"

"I don't give a damn."

Chapter 4

The sound of the phone ringing had awakened TeTe. She reached for it on the nightstand but couldn't find it. Half asleep, she sprang from her bed then spotted it under the bed. She grabbed the phone and saw that it was a missed call from Ms. Lucille, the nanny. She dialed the number back and Ms. Lucille was screaming frantically into the phone, saying someone had kidnapped Butterfly.

TeTe paced, she panted, and she ran her fingers through her hair. Did this old bitch just say that her daughter was missing? She had to be hearing her incorrectly.

Ms. Lucille was still yelling through the phone and saying Spanish words that TeTe did not understand. She did understand that if the bitch showed up at her house without her daughter, she was going to kill her ass.

"Calm down so I can understand you." TeTe said.

More Spanish words.

"Bitch, speak English."

"We were at the park playing, and all of a sudden this SUV pulls up. Two black men grabbed Butterfly and throws her in the SUV. And drives away."

"SUV? There are a thousand kinds of SUVS. What color

SUV?"

"It was black."

"What kind?"

"It was a Porsche, a really nice one."

TeTe sat down on the foot of the bed and said, "Let me get this shit straight: You let some men grab my daughter and throw her in a SUV?"

"Yes."

"And what the hell were you doing when this was going on?"

"Ms. Theresa, they had guns."

"I don't give a fuck what they had."

"I'm so sorry."

"Where are you?"

"I'm still at the park. I was going to call the police but I know how you feel about the police."

"Do not call the police," TeTe said. She dashed into her closet and found a pair of distressed jeans and she threw them across the bed.

"What do you want me to do?"

"Come to my house." TeTe hung the phone up then called Black. He didn't pick up. She then called him seven more times before he answered.

"I was trying to take a nap. Why are you blowing me up?"

"Look, my daughter has been kidnapped."

"What?"

"Yeah, she was at the park with the nanny and a black SUV pulled up and tossed her inside and drove off." TeTe slid into her jeans and a T-shirt. "I need you to come over right now."

"Give me thirty minutes."

"Okay."

An hour later Black came over. Eli was there and a goon named Caleb that TeTe had hired as her new enforcer along with John, TeTe's private investigator.

They were all assembled in the living room when Ms. Lucille rang the doorbell.

When TeTe opened the door, she grabbed Ms. Lucille by the hair and slung her to the floor and hit her with a flurry of punches.

"Get her off me!"

Black and Eli restrained TeTe.

TeTe said, "If anything happens to Butterfly, you're a dead old bitch."

Lucille rose to her feet. "It's not my fault."

TeTe said, "The hell if it's not your fault."

Black said," She did all she could do."

"Fuck you, black motherfucker."

"Being pissed at me is not going to bring Butterfly back. You don't even know who has her."

"What the fuck you mean, I don't know who has her?" TeTe closed her eyes briefly then opened them with a cold stare at the nanny. "It's those clowns from Detroit."

"You don't know that for sure."

TeTe turned to John. "What the fuck do you have on them? Were you able to find out where they live?"

"You killed the only person that knew where they were."

"I don't want to hear that shit. Can you find them or not?"

"I can, but it's taking more time than I thought."

The doorbell rang again.

She hurried over to the door.

A courier. A skinny white guy with red hair and freckles. His nametag read Dan. "I have a delivery for the owner of the house."

"That's me." TeTe snatched the goddamn pen from Dan's hand and signed her name on a pink piece of paper. He handed her the box.

Now what the fuck is in the box? she wondered. She would just die if it were one of Butterfly's body parts in the box. She ripped into the box and found an iPhone. She powered the phone on. There was only one contact: Butterfly. She dialed the number.

A man answered.

TeTe said, "Who the fuck is this?"

"Give me some respect now. I do have your daughter's life in my hands."

"What do you want from me?"

"I want us to be even."

"What are you talking about?"

"I don't hurt kids."

"Where is my daughter?"

The man laughed and said, "You see, it don't work like that. I'm not one of your hoes. You can't talk to me any kind of way."

"Where is my little girl?"

"She's safe."

"Let me speak to her."

Black snatched the phone from TeTe's hand and said, "Look, bruh, it's me that you want. I'm the one that had your brother killed."

"TeTe murdered my brother, so she has to pay."

"What do you want from us?"

"What the fuck do you think?"

"Money? How much do you need?"

"A million, and you will get Butterfly back in one piece. If not, you'll get her back in quite a few pieces."

"A million."

"You heard me, and you have exactly one week to get it to me. I'll send you the instructions on how to get the money to me."

TeTe wrestled with Black before regaining possession of the phone, but when she put the phone up to her ear, she heard a dial tone.

Chapter 5

A blunt of Bubba Kush dangled from the corner of Meeka's mouth when she opened the door for Brooke. Meeka said, "What can I do for you?"

"I'm looking for DeMontre."

Meeka inhaled the blunt and smiled. Her eyes damn near closed from the weed. She said, "You're that little girl that work for Starr?"

Brooke smiled. "Yes, ma'am."

Meeka invited Brooke inside. The scent from the fried chicken lingered. Meeka stubbed the blunt out on the kitchen table then placed it behind her ear. She turned to Brooke and said, "You hongry?"

"I've already eaten."

"You must don't like fried chicken."

"I love fried chicken."

"Well try my fried chicken." Meeka washed her hands in the kitchen sink, dried them, and handed Brooke a breast on a saucer. "You want some hot sauce?"

"I really don't like hot sauce."

"Girl, I put hot sauce on everything."

Brooke could believe that Meeka put hot sauce on

everything. Probably ate Sour Patch candy and was good at Double Dutch and made fun of girls who enunciated well, saying they acted white. So rather than getting accused of acting like she was better than Meeka, she would eat the fried chicken. She bit into the breast.

"How is it?"

Brooke said, "I love it." She held on tight to the chicken.

Meeka smiled and then said, "You look like you need to eat." Then she yelled, "Montre!"

"What, Mama?" The boy called out from the back room.

"Bring yo ass up here. You got company."

DeMontre arrived shirtless, his pants sagging. His brother, DeVante, followed him dressed the same, except he wore a wife beater.

DeMontre smiled when he saw Brooke. "I see Mama got you eating her chicken."

Brooke sat her plate down and licked her lips.

Meeka removed the blunt from behind her ear and lit it.

DeVante said, "Ma, let me hit the blunt."

Meeka stared at him and didn't answer.

"Don't be acting like that 'cuzMontre's little girlfriend over here."

"Montre?" Brooke said.

DeMontre said, "Mama and bro call me Montre for short."

Meeka passed DeVante the blunt. DeMontre grabbed Brooke's hand and they disappeared in the bedroom and closed the door.

"You have your own room?"

"You sound surprised."

"Do I?"

He laughed and said, "It's okay. I know you think that since I'm from the hood and shit, that I don't have nothing...and guess what?"

"What?"

"You are damn near accurate."

"I like your mom."

"She's cool. A lot different than auntie."

"Yeah, but I can tell they are sisters."

"They look alike."

"And they have the same energy."

"I guess."

DeMontre's room was small with a regular size bed. He plopped down on the bed and Brooke sat beside him.

She trembled as she traced his abs.

"What's wrong?"

"It's cold."

He sprang from the bed and grabbed her a Superman comforter.

She giggled when she saw it.

"You laughing at my comforter?"

"You're a little too big for Superman."

He frowned then walked back to the closet and tossed it back to the top.

"You're going to let me freeze?"

"Say you're sorry for picking at my comforter."

"Are you serious?"

He laughed then tossed the comforter to her.

She smiled at his sagging pants. When she was under the comforter she said, "Thanks."

"No problem. I can't have my woman being cold."

She grinned, revealing dimples. "I'm your woman?"

"You ate my Mama's fried chicken. That made it official."

She laughed and said, "Boy, you are too much."

He slid under the covers with her. His hands now resting on her ass.

She said, "Quit being bad; your mom is in there."

"In there getting faded with my brother."

"Damn, she is cool."

"Look, don't tell my auntie. Because she'll tell my grandma and 'em."

"And get your mom in trouble." She rubbed his thigh and his dick came alive.

He placed her hands on his piece and said, "You ready for this yet?"

"Almost."

He laughed and she situated herself on her side and rotated her ass toward him. His hands wrapped around her waist. She said, "I love you."

"I love you, too."

She turned and faced him and their noses touched. "I'm glad you came back home."

"I ain't have much of a choice. I had to get my mom to sign me out and she wanted me and my brother to come home. We all she has. Truth be told, I missed her."

"You a mama's boy?"

"I am."

"Ain't nothing wrong with that."

"Not in my book." He leaned forward and kissed her.

She smiled and said, "I was worried about you."

He laughed and said, "What, you didn't think I was going to get out?"

"I knew you were going to get out, silly."

"What were you worried about?"

"I don't know. I don't know what goes on in jail."

"I was only there for a day. Then my mama bonded me out."

She sat up on the bed, kicked her black Ugg boots off, and said, "Explain something to me?"

"What do you want to know?"

"How did drugs get under my car?"

"I dropped them when the police rolled up."

"Oh." She thought back to that night. She had almost gotten arrested.

He laughed and said, "I can still remember the look on your face when the police was questioning you."

"I didn't want to go to jail. Do you realize I could have had a criminal record?"

"Did you think I would let them take you?"

"No."

He put her hands on his dick again. And she rubbed it. Her legs moistened.

She removed his dick then gasped, "Your mama is in the next room."

"You've made that point already, shawty."

He made his way to the door and locked it. He assumed his same position back on the bed. His dick still exposed. He placed her hand on it again and she stroked it. He pushed her head forward and her lips grazed it. She gazed at him while her hands wrapped around the base of his dick.

She said, "I've never done this."

"I know. It's going to be okay."

"The door is locked, right?"

"You going to do it or not?"

"I am." She took him deep inside her mouth.

Chapter 6

There were two conversations that Starr didn't want to have. The first one was to tell Q that she wasn't pregnant by him, and the other was telling Terrell that he was the father of her baby. She drove to Terrell's neighborhood then reconsidered. She called Jada.

"Girl, I'm in Terrell's neighborhood."

"Who?"

"The basketball player."

"Your baby daddy?"

"I guess you can say that."

"What's up?"

Starr pulled her car over to the side of the road. "I need you to talk me into going to his house. I don't know how this is going to go, Jada. I don't know what he is going to say. What he is going to do? Is he going to want me to keep the baby? If he is going to want me to get rid of the baby. There are just so many thoughts running through my head."

"I honestly don't think you should tell him, but I know you will," Jada said.

"You are right. I'm not going to be able to live with myself if I don't tell him."

"Well, don't think about it. Just drive to his driveway and get out before you can think about it too hard. Jump out and run up to the door. Ring the bell and when he opens the door tell him you're pregnant."

"Just like that?"

"That simple."

"What do you think he's going to say?"

"He's probably going to ask why the hell you even bothering to tell him, if you are going to kill the baby."

Hearing Jada put it that bluntly gave Starr more confidence. "Thanks, girl."

"I'll stay on the phone with you if you want."

"I can handle it myself." Starr fired up the ignition and drove up to his driveway.

Lights were on in the den. Perhaps he was watching the game with his friends. She was thinking again, and she didn't need to do that. She parked the car and marched right up to the porch, stood on the welcome mat, and rang the doorbell.

The door swung open and a young Hispanic woman appeared with green eyes, flowing hair, and a ridiculous amount of hips and ass. Quads popping through neon green spandex went well with a midriff and a sports bra that revealed chiseled abs. A younger, sluttier version of J-Lo.

"Can I help you?" J-Ho said.

Starr's lips trembled, thinking that this bitch spent her time between the gym and the plastic surgeon's office. She was the typical athlete's woman. "Is Terrell here?"

"Yes. I'll get him. What's your name, honey?" J-Ho smiled.

She wanted to tell her that her name was Baby Mama. If she said that, she would wreck J-Ho's world.

"Tell him that Ms. Coleman, the interior decorator, is here. Tell him I misplaced a check that he had given me a few weeks ago."

J-Ho disappeared inside the house and trotted upstairs. Starr looked at that perfect ass bouncing up the stairs.

Terrell rushed downstairs. He looked damn good with radiant skin and sparkling white teeth. Why in the hell didn't she want to give this man a chance again?

J-Ho stood at his side and held his arm, her face saying, get your own millionaire; this one is mine.

Terrell said, "Ms. Coleman, good to see you. Carmen tells me you had a problem with the check."

"Yeah."

Terrell made eye contact with J-Ho and said, "Can I talk to Ms. Coleman for a moment?" He invited Starr inside and led her to the den and closed the door.

"You moved on without me extremely fast."

He smiled and said, "Look, you didn't want to be with me. What the hell was I supposed to do, just sit here and wait on you?"

"No. But damn that was fast. Did you get her out of the strip club?"

"Black women love to throw shade when a black man is happy."

"I ain't hardly throwing shade, nigga." Starr sighed. Thinking there was no way she was going to tell him that she was pregnant. "I was in the neighborhood."

"Why didn't you call?"

"I don't know." She stood and made a break for the door, but he blocked her. She turned and spotted the TV that she had convinced him to buy months earlier. Her face looked sad and he asked was she okay.

"No."

"What's wrong?"

"Does she watch the TV?"

He looked confused.

"Does little J-Ho watch the TV that I picked out for you?"

"Are you jealous?"

She was kind of jealous. Kind of sad that he had moved on so fast, but she wouldn't let him know.

He caressed her hand. "What's wrong?"

"Nothing." He released her hand and she asked him. "Do you like her?"

"What? I do."

"Okay, well, there's nothing to talk about."

Terrell said, "Look, Starr, I tried my best to get with you and you didn't want me. You made it clear that you didn't want me and I had to accept it."

She smiled a fake smile and said, "So you moved on?"

"I did."

"And she makes you happy?"

"She does."

Starr extended her hand out to him and he took it inside his and said, "If she makes you happy, there is nothing to talk about."

"This is fucked up."

"Why is it fucked up? You're happy."

"I don't know." He sighed and said, "Part of me wants you, but I know that I wasn't your first choice, and I know I could never be your first choice and that would bother me."

Starr said, "Can you move so I can go home? I have a child I have to go home to."

He stepped aside and Starr exited the room. Ms. J-Ho was outside doing some sort of lunge exercise. Her ass looking more pronounced than ever, and Starr figured that was all she was good for. A gold digger with a very nice ass. She stared at Starr then smiled.

Starr finally made her way to her car. She dropped her head on the steering wheel and cried. She was pregnant and alone.

• • •

Starr drove to Jada's home. When Jada saw Starr's face she knew she had been crying. She hugged her and invited her in. "What happened?" Jada asked.

"I couldn't tell him."

"Couldn't tell who?"

"Terrell."

Jada frowned. "Starr you didn't tell him?"

"No."

"Why not?"

"He had a girl over. Some hispanic J-Lo looking girl. Looked liked she spent all day at the squat rack. You know the Instagram Thot type." Starr said before realizing that Jada was that type with hundreds of thousands of followers.

"What about her?"

"He looked happy with her and I just didn't want to ruin it for them."

"Look Starr, if you're going to abort the baby. Why does he have to know? You always want to do the right thing and look where it got you."

"I know."

"What are you going to do?"

"I don't know."

"Look I know I shouldn't be telling you this, but I feel bad trying to hide this from you."

"Hide what?"

"Its about Q."

"What about Q?"

"Do you remember that girl Shantelle?"

"Who?"

"The girl I beat the brakes off at Trey's funeral."

Starr laughed remembering the fight. "Trey's Jump off?"

"Yeah her."

"What about her?"

"I saw her at Lennox a few weeks ago and she spoke to me. I didn't recognize her at first. I thought she was coming back for some revenge and I was about to beat that ass again, but she was peaceful."

"Ok, Jada get to the point."

"She told me some crazy shit. She had told me that Q had brought some Mexicans to kill Trey before Jessica killed him."

"What? I don't believe her."

"Look you should at least hear her out." Starr said. "This is just too much for me to take." She lowered her head and began to cry.

Chapter 7

Brooke disappeared to inform Starr that Q was there to see
her. Seconds later, she returned and told Q that Starr
wanted him to come on back.

Starr was sitting at her desk when he entered the office.
She picked up the phone and called to the front of the studio
to tell Brooke that she could take the rest of the day off.

"You shutting down early?"

"No."

Q took a seat in the chair across from her desk then asked,
"Mind if I have a seat?"

"You're already seated."

He smiled and said, "You seem annoyed."

"A lot is going on with me."

"I've called you about ten times and you didn't answer."

"I'm sorry." She picked her phone up and checked her
Instagram. A pic of Jada was coming down her newsfeed. A
thirst trap. She was wearing an alluring black leotard that
revealed her entire ass. Sixteen thousand likes. For the first
time, she was envious of Jada, who was carefree and fucked
whomever she wanted, whenever she wanted. Posted thirst
traps. Used men for money. Yeah, but she wasn't pregnant

by a man that was with another woman. Nor did she have to break the it's-not-your-baby news to the man she loved. She had tried to do everything the right way. She was proud that she had morals and values, but what good did that do? She still found herself in a very compromising situation.

She liked Jada's picture and set her phone back down.

"What is it you want to say to me?" Q asked.

"What makes you say that?"

He locked eyes with her and said, "You aborted my baby, didn't you?"

There was an awkward silence.

Q stood and paced. "How could you do a thing like that? How in the fuck did you abort my child without letting me know that you were going to do it?"

He was already seated on page 30.

"I didn't abort the baby."

He sat down then he looked at her with pleading eyes and said, "What's wrong?"

"There is no baby."

"You lied?"

"No." She looked away. "I didn't lie."

"What do you mean there is no baby?"

"Well, there is no baby for you."

"What? I don't understand."

"Q, I'm not pregnant by you."

He sat silent for a moment. His heart beating with irregularity. "What the fuck are you talking about?"

"I'm pregnant by the basketball player."

"What?"

"Yeah, I went to the ob-gyn and found out how far along I am." She paused. "The math is pointing to him."

Q was breathing hard as hell.

"I'm sorry."

Q dropped his head between his legs. His leg trembled and he said, "You mean to tell me that you're carrying another man's seed?"

"I'm sorry."

"You are carrying another man's baby?"

"I didn't mean for this to happen."

"You fucked him. You knew it could happen."

He stood and was about to rush for the door and she stopped him.

"Get the fuck out of my way."

"I'm not going to have the baby."

"Why?"

"What do you mean why? I told you when I thought it was yours that I may not have it."

"Does he know?"

"He doesn't."

"You didn't tell him?"

She stepped aside and sat back down.

He turned then sat back across from her and said, "Why didn't you tell him?"

"I couldn't." Her voice was very weak.

"That is wrong on so many levels."

"I know." She avoided eye contact with him and picked up the phone to skim through Jada's Instagram. Lots of restaurant pics. Pics of steak and lobster. Always at a five-star restaurant. And pictures of her pretending to be working out at the gym, including four selfies that damn near looked the same.

Starr sighed and said, "I couldn't tell him."

"Why not?"

"I knocked on his door with every intention on telling him, but some J-Lo-looking bitch with a big ass answered the door."

"You like him, don't you?"

"No, that's just it."

"Sounds like you're jealous of the J-Lo-looking bitch."

"I am not jealous of the bitch. I was just telling you what happened."

"Was she his girlfriend?"

"Yeah."

Q chuckled and this pissed Starr off.

"It's not funny."

He stood and walked around in a circle with his hands underneath his chin, pondering. "I don't understand this shit at all. I mean, you have a man that really wants you, and you want to take a break? But you really wanted to run around and fuck some athlete but lie to me like you wanted to take a break. Now you're pregnant by a man that don't even want your ass."

She picked up a picture frame and slung it at his ass and it barely missed his head.

"What the hell was that all about?"

"First of all, Q, it's your fault I'm in this situation. If you hadn't lied like you fucked that Chanel chick, we wouldn't be here right now."

"But we are here."

"So you admit that you fucked her?"

"I never fucked her. I cut her off. Deleted her number out of my phone. Bitch was too high and mighty for me. Now we're here, you pregnant and I still love you."

"What do you want to do about that?"

"You're the one that's pregnant."

"I know." She cried. Q rushed by her side and she looked up and made eye contact with him and said, "I don't know what to do."

The phone rang. She picked it up and said. "Jada I'm going to have to call you back."

She ended the call and said. "Which reminds me did you want to pay some Mexicans to kill Trey?"

"What?" Q sounded surprised. "Where the fuck is that coming from?"

"Just answer the question?"

"Wait a minute did Jada tell you that?"

"Why would she tell me that? How would she know?"

"You said before you asked me, that her call reminded you of that?"

"Look Q answer the question?"

"Hell No." Then he stormed out of her office.

Chapter 8

Q showed up at Fresh's place unannounced. A stripper with a long, wavy weave opened the door and Q said, "Where the fuck is Fresh?"

Fresh appeared shirtless wearing boxer briefs. He was brushing his teeth.

"I need to talk to you."

Fresh signaled for the unidentified woman to give him privacy. He kept brushing his teeth as he made his way to the kitchen sink. He spat toothpaste in the sink and said, "What's wrong?"

"What's wrong is what you told Jada."

Q began to pace and Fresh watched him.

"What are you talking about, bruh?"

Q stopped and faced Fresh. "What I'm talking about is you told Jada that I wanted to have Trey killed."

"What?"

Q's face became serious. "Look, you don't have to lie. I know you told Jada this."

"I ain't tell nobody shit, bruh!"

Q opened the fridge and grabbed a Fanta grape soda. Popped the top and asked Fresh, "Why did you tell her, bruh?"

"I didn't tell nobody shit."

"How did Starr find out?"

"Jada."

"Who told Jada?"

"It damn sure wasn't me," Fresh said. Then he thought back to the day when Jada asked him about whether Q wanted Trey dead. "Listen, this is what happened."

"Tell me." Q took another swig of the soda and made eye contact with Fresh.

"Jada told me about some girl that she had seen at the mall. I don't know who the bitch is, but she supposedly approached Jada and told her that you had wanted Trey dead."

Q laughed and said, "You think I'm supposed to believe that shit?"

"I don't give a damn about what you believe. This is the truth, bruh. I ain't gotta lie."

"So this girl approached Jada at the mall and says that I wanted to have Trey killed?"

"Yeah. I think she was Trey's side bitch or something."

"How does she look?"

"I didn't see her. Jada told me all about it. I wasn't with Jada at the mall. Jada came over here and asked me about it, and I told her not to mention it again."

"That little bitch."

"Do you know who I am talking about?"

Q drank the rest of the soda and burped. "Yeah. I know her."

"Who is she?"

"This girl name Shantelle."

"Shantelle?"

"She came down a few times with Trey."

"She knows?"

"She does."

Fresh said, "You owe me an apology."

"I'm sorry."

"So what's next?"

"I don't know. I don't know."

• • •

When Fresh entered Jada's home, she offered him something to drink. He declined and she offered him a seat.

"I won't be long," he said.

"Okay, I'm not understanding. What brings you over here?"

"Look, you told Starr what I told you not to tell her!"

Jada looked at his silly ass. Was this motherfucker trying to get loud? Did he come to her house to show out? He didn't want her to start showing out. She inched toward him.

"First of all, calm the fuck down," she said.

"Why, Jada?"

"Why what, motherfucker?"

"Why did you tell her?"

"She deserved to know."

"I can't believe you."

Jada's hands rested on her hips. "You told Q that she was pregnant, and I told you not to say nothing."

"That's different."

"How is it different?"

"Because that man needed to know she was carrying his baby."

"Fresh, don't come in my house with no bullshit."

"I wished you hadn't told her that."

"Well, if he deserved to know that he might be a father, she deserved to know that Q wanted Trey dead."

"Might be a father? What do you mean, might be? She's having an abortion?"

"I don't know, that's between Starr and Q." Jada almost revealed to Fresh that Q wasn't the father. She didn't want to get pulled into this mess any more than she was already in it. That would have to be a conversation between Starr and Q.

Fresh pulled Jada closer and she broke free from his grip.

He said, "I was just looking out for my homie."

"And I was protecting Starr."

He headed for the door, and when he was about to open the door, the bell rang. She stepped ahead of him and opened the door. Tank stood there and Fresh gave him a once-over. The man looked like he spent a lot of time in the gym. And there was a gun print at his waist.

Jada hugged him.

Tank and Fresh stared at each other for a while and there was an awkward silence.

Jada said, "Fresh, this is my baby, Tank."

Fresh extended his hand and said, "I'm a friend of her friend's ex."

Jada said, "Why lie?" Then she made eye contact with Tank and said, "We used to fuck. He came over because he's pissed that I told my friend something about his boy."

"So you came over for that?"

"Whatever she and I had, it's over."

Tank said, "I know damn well it's over, and after today, don't bring yo ass over here again."

"And if I do?"

Tank raised his T-shirt to reveal a black .45 handgun. "We're gonna have problems."

Fresh made eye contact with Tank. Ever since the day he'd been caught with guns, he would ride around unarmed. Jada sensed the tension and wedged herself between the two of them.

She turned to Fresh and said, "Go."

Tank gritted his teeth. "Yeah, nigga, leave."

Chapter 9

Inside a Waffle House in Cobb County, Black and Daniels sat in a corner booth. Black chomped down on pecan waffles while Daniels had a cup of coffee.

"So what happened to Bird?" Black asked as he gulped orange juice.

Daniels shrugged. "I don't know."

"You don't know?" Black eyed him suspiciously.

"Let's just say I dropped him off."

"Where?"

"Dropped him off on a dirt road in Forsyth County."

You think he made it out of there alive?"

"No idea." Daniels tasted the coffee and decided that he needed another sugar. He added two more. "Can we talk about something else?"

"Did you get my money back?"

"I did."

"Where is it?"

"It's in the car. I'll give it to you when we leave."

"It's all there?"

"Of course, but I'm taking ten percent of it."

"This is why I asked was it all there."

"I did the favor. I got the money back."

"I understand." Black's face got serious. "I really need your help again."

"What now?"

"Girlfriend's daughter got kidnapped."

"And what can I do about that?"

"They're asking for a million dollars and they'll give her back."

"What are you asking me?"

"I need to get the money from you."

"A million dollars? I don't have that kind of cash laying around."

"You're the FBI."

"FBI, not U.S. Treasury."

"You gotta help me."

"Black, the deal we made was that I keep Homeland Security off your ass and we work together as partners. The deal wasn't that I go behind you and clean up all your shit. I got your money from Bird, and now you want me to do this?"

"Keep the money you got from Bird and keep anything that you might give me. You don't want to help me, I don't wanna help you."

Daniels became angry. "You can't be serious."

"This little girl means the world to me, and if you can help me..."

"I can't help you. It's simple. Where am I supposed to get a million dollars from?"

"I got half."

"I can assemble a team of agents to get the little girl back. Get a hostage negotiator and all."

"This ain't going to end up good if we go that route."

"Remember, you just gave Bird a shitload of money, and he reneged on his deal. What make you think the people who took the girl are any different?"

"But I had a feeling he was going to renege."

"How do we know that these dudes are going to give the girl back if we give them the money?"

"We don't."

Daniels thought about it then finally smiled. "I'm going to help you."

• • •

After a quick bite to eat, Q and Diego had a much-needed conversation.

"You want to tell me what's going on with you and Fresh?" Diego asked.

"Nothing."

"But you're keeping secrets."

"I have my reasons."

"I only want to deal with you, so it's okay."

"I already know that." Q traded stares with him.

"Can you cut Gordo off?"

"You don't own me."

"I can give you enough product. The same product."

"I gave you too much power before and when I wanted to walk away, you killed my friend."

"Old news."

"His family want you dead. People in the streets of Houston want you dead."

"You want to tell me something that I don't know?"

Q laughed. Lots of people wanted Diego dead and that didn't seem to faze him.

"I think I understand now." He downed the remainder of his drink and said, "You don't want Fresh to know that you are dealing with me because the word might get out, and it might damage your reputation."

"Exactly."

"I understand, my friend."

"This cannot get out."

"You don't trust me?"

"Why should I trust you?"

"Look, Q, I don't want to risk it. I don't want to lose your business."

The two men touched fists.

Chapter 10

Jada hugged Starr as soon as she entered her home and asked, "Girl, what you got in here to drink?"

"Soda, water, juice. What do you want?"

"None of the above. I need a real drink."

"There is Ciroc in the liquor cabinet, and some Sprite."

Jada poured a glass of Ciroc then headed into the living room. They both sat on the sofa at opposite ends. Jada took a swig of her drink and said, "I was just coming by to check on you. The last time we spoke you seemed like you were in a bad space."

"I was. I'm better now."

"You must be relieved."

"Not at all." Starr stood and paced. She stopped and turned toward Jada.

Jada said, "What happened?"

"Nothing happened. I just couldn't bring myself to tell him."

"So you're going to do what I suggested in the first place?"

"I don't know what I should do."

"You want the baby?"

"I do...but I don't. I'm so confused."

Jada sipped her drink and said, "I have to ask...and don't get mad at me for asking."

"Ask me any damn thing you want."

"Do you want to be with him?"

"Not at all. I thought I wanted Q. And Terrell seemed so happy to be with that woman, but he said if I would give him a chance, he would get rid of her."

"Well damn."

"I couldn't do it, Jada. I don't want him. I couldn't tell him that I was pregnant then abort his baby."

Jada set her drink down and ran to Starr's side. She hugged her and said, "I just want you to know that I'm here for you."

"I know."

Jada took her position back on the sofa.

"I told Q that the baby wasn't his."

"What did he say?"

"He was pissed at first. Then he calmed down. I confronted him about wanting to kill Trey."

"And?"

"He denied it."

"I ain't got to lie," Jada said. "I can call that Shantelle right now, and she'll tell you the same thing that she told me and Fresh didn't deny it."

"I believe you."

"Bitch-ass Fresh came over my house trying to ask me why I told you what I knew."

"What?"

"Yeah, he came over asking me why I told you."

"Why did he ask you that?"

"Because at first..." Jada gulped down the Cîroc and then poured another glass. "Like I was saying at first, I didn't know if I was going to tell you or not."

"Why wouldn't you tell me this? Why wouldn't you think that I would want to know?"

"It's not that I didn't think I should tell you. I thought that you and Q would get back together and that would be that. Besides, he didn't kill Trey; that crazy bitch did."

"Yeah, I guess you're right, but you know how much Trey meant to me. You know how I loved that man."

"Yeah, but he's not here."

"He's not here and I'm pregnant and alone," Starr said in the saddest voice.

"You're not alone. Auntie Jada is here, and you have your family to support you. A loving family."

"I don't know what I should do."

Chapter 11

BROOKE TOOK DEMONTRE DEEP INSIDE HER MOUTH AND sucked him aggressively.

He shoved her and said, "Too much teeth, shawty."

She smiled, looking sexy with her hair pulled back and held with a scrunchie. Saliva cascaded down her jaw. "I love sucking you, Montre."

"You trying to sound hood?"

"No. Not at all. I'm trying to make you happy." She stroked his penis.

"I'm real happy. I'd be even happier if you let me inside you."

"You know I can't do that."

"So let me get this straight. You don't mind giving head, but you don't want me inside you?"

"I love making you feel good."

He laughed and said, "That's the craziest shit I ever heard of."

"All of my friends have given blowjobs, but all of us are virgins."

"Blowjobs?" He laughed and said, "That's so old school, so white-sounding. But let me guess; your friends that like to give blowjobs are black girls that sound white."

"That's what you would probably want to call them."

He sat up on the bed, zipped his pants up, and said, "Why can't you just let me put it in for like a minute? We can time it. A minute. I will take it out in a minute, I promise."

She folded her arms. "Look I want to go to college. My parents would be so disappointed if I got pregnant."

"You're not going to get pregnant."

"Why did you say that?"

"I've never gotten anyone pregnant before."

"You're going to put it in for one minute and then take it out?"

"I promise."

"Won't I bleed if you put it in? I don't want to bleed."

"You won't bleed. I can promise you that you won't bleed."

"Will it hurt?"

"No."

They both slid out of their clothes. His dick hanging. Not fully erect. She trembled before she heard a loud bang on the door. They both scrambled to put their clothes on. She slid into her pants. Her bra was nowhere to be found, so he tossed her a blanket.

"What the hell y'all doing in there?" Meeka yelled. "Open this damn do', Montre."

"Hold up, Ma." DeMontre slid into his bedroom shoes and said to Brooke, "Just pretend you're asleep."

DeMontre opened the door and Meeka stepped inside "What the fuck y'all doing in here?"

DeMontre put his hands over her mouth and said, "She's asleep. She ain't feeling good."

"What do you mean she's asleep?"

"She not feeling well. Cramps."

"Oh, the lil heifer on her period? Good. At least I know there ain'tgonna be no babies around here. I'm too damn fly to be a grandma. You hear me, boy?"

"Ain'tnobody even doing nothing. I was just rubbing her shoulders as she sleep."

Brooke was lying in the bed looking so peaceful.

Meeka said, "I like that little girl. She seems so sweet."

"She's a really nice girl."

"What she doing with yo ass?"

"Come on, Ma." DeMontre laughed.

"I'm just saying."

"Saying what?"

"Nigga, you overachieved this time."

"Whatever."

"Whatever, my ass. Don't you close that damn door. You ain't making no baby in my house."

"Stop it, Ma."

"If you close that door again, I swear I'm going to get her parents' phone number from Starr."

"Quit tripping, Ma."

Chapter 12

A strange white man sat in TeTe's living room. He was tall and skinny with wire-framed glasses, and he was slightly humpbacked. The man studied Black and Black frowned.

TeTe said, "Mark, this is my husband."

Black reached out and they shook hands.

TeTe said, "Mark is a client. He wants to take two of the girls on a month-long business trip to Hong Kong."

"Oh really?"

"Yes."

"Mark excuse me for a moment." Her and Black walked into the next room

"Okay, he wants girls, but why the fuck is he here?"

TeTe looked at Black with serious eyes. "I'm going to sell my cars."

"What?"

"I have to come up with the money. I have to get my daughter from these clowns. I gotta do what I gotta do, understand me?"

"He's going to pay you cash?"

"This is what I'm trying to get him to do."

"You're not going to sell your shit."

"I don't have the money and I can't let these motherfuckers hurt my daughter. If something happens to Butterfly, I don't know what I am going to do."

"Nothing is going to happen to Butterfly."

"Black, I ain't trying to hear this shit unless you got the money."

"I have the money."

"Are you serious?"

"I have the money, babe. And we're going to get Butterfly back, I promise."

She hugged Black. "I don't know how I'm going to make this up to you."

He cupped her ass.

She slapped his hand away playfully and said, "You're so fucking nasty." She let him go and told him about another package she'd received from the courier, which included another phone and instructions for her to call.

"Did you call him?"

"Yeah."

"And what did he say?"

"He wanted a hundred thousand dollars by the end of the day."

"I'll get it to you."

"I sent it already."

"How?"

"The same courier company. They arranged it."

"I wish you hadn't done that. The next time you hear from them again, let me know before you do anything."

"Well, they want the rest of the money by the end of the week."

"You sure she's okay?"

"FaceTimed her."

"And she's okay? Are you sure?"

"She appeared to be fine."

"Great."

"Black, I love you."

There was an awkward silence and finally he said, "I love you too."

• • •

Tank and Jada met at Capital Grill for food and drinks. She had noticed that he had been acting strangely ever since the day he met Fresh. They ordered their food and he was playing with his phone when she said, "So are you going to talk to me or not?"

He placed his phone on the table and said, "What do you want to talk about?"

"I wanna know why you haven't been talking to me lately?"

He smiled. "I'm here, ain't I?"

She bit her lip. "You know what I'm talking about."

"I don't."

"You barely said a word for the last week, and every time I text you, it's the one-word responses. I am surprised that you even agreed to come out tonight."

"Be honest with me."

She finished the soda and shook the ice in the cup. "About what?"

"What's going on with you and this Fresh character?"

"He's somebody I used to fuck around with. Nothing more."

"A fuck buddy?"

"A fuck buddy. A Netflix and chill buddy. But that's about it."

"So have you fucked him since we have been together?"

"What difference does it make?"

"Have you?"

"I have."

"Damn, Jada."

"Come on, Tank, it's not like you are being real with me. You have a woman. Let me remind you of that."

"You just did. You fucked him raw?"

"No," she lied.

Tank huffed then picked up his phone again.

Jada said, "Wait a goddamn minute! If you're going to act like this, we may as well end this shit right now."

"Is it wrong for me to want you all to myself?"

"That can never happen."

Tank looked at her with serious eyes and said, "Why not?

You don't like me?"

"No, babe." She rubbed his chest. "It's not that at all. It's just that you have a woman, and I don't mind playing number two but if you want me to cut off people, you're going to have to cut her off too. I'm eventually trying to be somebody's wife."

Silence.

"You trying to go to the next level?" she asked.

"What next level?"

Jada stared at his dumb ass. He knew damn well what she was asking. "You know what I'm talking about. Are you ready to commit to only me?"

"I am."

"What about her? You're going to leave her?"

"I will."

Jada didn't expect him to say that but she was glad he did. She didn't know if he was lying or not, but it was good to see somebody taking her seriously. She liked Tank and he was definitely the kind of man that she could see herself with.

Chapter 13

The scent of McDonald's fries hit Q as soon as he entered Starr's home. He watched her walk away from him and scurry into the living room with a McDonald's bag in her hand. She plopped down and forked out a handful of fries from the bag, tossed them in her mouth, then guzzled down a cup of Coke that sat on the table. A cheeseburger leaking ketchup was on the table. More ketchup was waiting in a paper container. "Are you coming in here, or are you going to stand there looking like a statue?"

He sat across from her. "What's going on?"

"You tell me." She watched him.

"Junk food?"

"Pregnant food."

"Are you having cravings for bad food or is this an excuse to eat it?"

"What the hell did you come over here for, Q?" She rolled her eyes then dipped her cheeseburger into more ketchup.

"I came to say I shouldn't have stormed out."

"You act like a goddamn thirteen-year-old sometimes."

"I know and I'm sorry." He stood and grabbed a couple of her fries and dabbed them into the ketchup.

When he sat back down he said, "I know I shouldn't have left out."

"Without answering my question?"

"Question?"

"You know damn well what I'm talking about."

"Do we have to talk about that?"

"Q, did you or did you not want to have Trey dead?"

"It's not that simple."

"Yes, it is."

Q stood and paced, his back now away from her. He stopped and looked at her and said, "Trey got busted."

"What are you talking about?"

"He got stopped in Louisiana."

"He told me about that."

"He did?"

"Yes." Starr grabbed another cheeseburger from the bag. She smelled onions, and she had asked for no onions. Dumb-ass cashier with the red braids probably didn't take her order correctly. She scraped the onions from the top of the burger. "Yes, he told me the police stopped him and took his money and let him go."

"And you believed him?"

"Why would he lie to me?"

"Did you know he was with another bitch?" he asked.

"I did." She bit into the burger and said, "So you making this about me and him. Where are you going with this? Did you try to have Trey murdered or not?"

He sat back down and said, "Not exactly."

"What do that mean?"

"I thought about it. That's just how the game goes. You know, Starr, I thought—"

"You thought he had been busted and that he was going to tell on you."

"I did."

"So you wanted to kill him?"

"I did. I went to someone and was going to have them take him out. But fortunately for me, I didn't have to do that."

Tears rolled down Starr's face.

"Don't cry."

She balled the bag of food up and tossed it, smacking him in the face.

"I'm sorry."

"I can't believe you. You ain't shit, Q." She suddenly rushed him, hitting him with a flurry of blows to the chest and face.

He grabbed her hands and restrained her. As he was holding her hands, she kicked him in the groin.

"Let me go."

He held her tightly and forced her to look at him. "This is why I wanted out, Starr."

"You're nothing but a liar."

"Do you realize what the game has done do me? I hate what I became. This is why I wanted one of my best friends dead, and I wanted out because of it."

"You ain't shit, Q. Get the fuck out of my house."

"I'm not going."

"Motherfucker, I will scream rape as loud as I can. Go, Q!"

"I ain't kill Trey; the crazy bitch killed Trey."

"She killed him before you could get to him."

Q approached her and she attempted to kick him again. He blocked her feet then grabbed her. She screamed. He covered her mouth and the tears began to well in her eyes.

He said, "I'm not going to let you go, and you're going to have this baby. I'm going to raise it like it's my own. I love you and I don't want to ever be out of your life. I want to raise T.J. and the new baby. I want you. I want to make a family with you. I forgive you for getting pregnant by somebody else. I just need you to forgive me for what I wanted to do with Trey."

He uncovered her mouth and placed his lips over hers. She tried to scream but she couldn't. He kissed her and she tried to push him away. He was too strong, so finally she didn't resist.

• • •

Dan the courier came with a new package and TeTe signed for it. A new phone. TeTe powered it up then it rang. "Hello."

"Time is running out, bitch."

"Where the fuck is my daughter?"

"Don't worry about her."

"Let me speak to her."

"You don't tell me what the fuck to do. I tell you what the fuck to do. Get that money!"

"I have the goddamn money!"

Seconds later, Butterfly said, "Hello?"

"You okay?"

"I'm fine, Mom. I just ate pizza and I've been playing with Ciara."

"Who is that?"

The kidnapper snatched the phone from Butterfly's hand. "She's been playing with my daughter. She's ten."

"Okay, what do you want me to do?"

There is a note taped to the bottom of the box. Underneath a piece of cloth. Read the letter and follow the instructions."

"But—"

The call dropped, terminated.

The note was on a piece of yellow notebook paper.

TeTe said to John, "I want you to go get my daughter."

"You know I will."

After considering something, TeTe said, "That's okay; I'll get someone else to do it."

"Why?"

"Just never mind, John."

John laughed and said, "Wait a minute. If you think I'm going to touch your daughter, you are out of your fuckin mind. I like women."

TeTe gave him a side eye. "John, you like girls."

"Eighteen and older. Besides, you'll kill me."

"You goddamn right I'll have you murdered. As long as you know this."

"I've known Butterfly since she was a baby. I want to do this. I want to help out."

"Okay. You will have to meet the woman at Panera Bread on Chastain Road at eight o'clock. You are going to take the money in these two briefcases. You are to pass the money to a woman wearing a blue pinstriped pants suit. She's kind of short with long natural hair. She will take the briefcase then verify that the money is inside. After she verifies, a man wearing a blue North Face jacket will enter the restaurant, and he's going to release Butterfly to you. You understand?"

"I do."

"Do you have a gun?"

"Do I need a gun? We'll be in a public place."

"I don't give a fuck. I want you to shoot that bitch if she try anything funny."

John was face to face with TeTe, who wasn't flinching. He knew she meant it. He would have to take his gun.

Chapter 14

LATER THAT NIGHT, JOHN MADE THE EXCHANGE WITHOUT incident and returned Butterfly back to TeTe.

"Oh my God, my baby is home!"

TeTe planted kisses on her daughter's face. Butterfly was happy to see her mother.

Then TeTe frowned. "What the hell are you wearing?"

"I'm wearing some of Ciara's clothes. She is a little bigger than me."

"Well, go upstairs and take a shower and change your clothes."

Butterfly dashed halfway up the stairs before stopping and looking back. "I love you, Mom."

"I love you, too, baby."

TeTe hugged John and said, "Thanks."

The doorbell rang.

It was Black. TeTe let him in and he said, "Is she home?"

"She's home."

"Tell her to come downstairs."

"She's taking a shower right now. She'll be down in a few."

Black was smiling as TeTe moved closer and hugged him.

"Thank you, baby. I'm so happy that my baby is home, and

I promise I'm going to make it up to you."

Black released her from his grip. He looked down and gripped her ass again and said, "I look at Butterfly like she's my daughter."

"I'm just so happy that she is home. I thought I was going to go crazy."

"She's home now and we're going to celebrate."

"How?"

"We're going to take Butterfly out and, after dinner, we'll come back and have our own private celebration."

•   •   •

Her name was Morgan Davies but her friends called her The Body. Morgan was from Macon, Georgia. She had thick, full eyebrows and hair that flowed down to an ass that could rival a mule's. Morgan's job was to look amazing while the local dope boys spoiled her. Her latest man had just given her 8,000 dollars in cash, most of which she had used to pay her daughter's private school tuition. Today she would do a little shopping in Phipps. She would buy herself the Louis Vuitton Kimono bag.

As Morgan left the Louis store, she noticed two white men tailing her. It wasn't unusual. Men followed her all the time; sometimes they would speak and sometimes they wouldn't. But it wasn't unusual for the white ones not to speak. They wanted black women, but some just didn't know how to approach a black woman, so they would follow her, which was always downright creepy.

She felt them getting closer to her and it was making her nervous. She stopped in her tracks and that's when one of the men, the shorter one with dark hair and a mustache, flashed credentials. "Secret Service."

"What?" She laughed and kept walking.

"I'm not playing, ma'am. Stop."

She stopped and turned to face the man and his partner.

The partner was taller but also had dark hair, a tan, and was more attractive. Looked to be in his early thirties. Good looking but in a country boy kind of way.

The tall one introduced himself as Agent Adam Cooper.

"What the fuck do you want with me?"

Ma'am, we're not going to embarrass you," Cooper said then put her at ease. "Could you please follow us?"

Morgan said, "Tell me what this is about?"

The short guy said, "Follow us or we're going to have to put you in cuffs."

"Put me in cuffs for what? I ain't even done shit."

Cooper said, "We'll sort everything out in the mall security office."

"Mall security? I ain't stole nothing. I paid for this bag. In cash. I got the receipt." She flashed the receipt.

"Follow us, ma'am."

Morgan reluctantly followed the two men until they reached the security room. There was an old black security guard named Burt. Cooper asked Burt to give them fifteen minutes alone with her.

"Sure," Burt said and tossed him the keys. "Just lock up the place when you're done. I'll be standing over by the food court. You can just bring the keys to me there."

Cooper thanked Burt. When Burt was gone, Cooper sat behind the desk that had a couple of monitors sitting on it. Morgan sat in the aluminum chair across from Cooper. The short guy kept glancing at Morgan's thighs.

"What's going on?"

"You paid for your bag?"

"I did."

"With cash?"

"Yes. That's not against the law."

"Hundreds and fifties?"

"Yes."

"Can I see one?"

"One what?"

"Do you have another hundred- or fifty-dollar bill on you?"

"I do." She dug into her purse and passed him a fifty-dollar bill.

Cooper examined the bill. "Ms. Davies, this bill is counterfeit."

"What? I had no idea."

"We believe you."

"You do?"

"Yes."

"Why am I here then?" She crossed her legs.

"Because we want to know where you got it from," Cooper said. His crystal blue eyes so intense she could just melt. He was the kind of white boy that she would certainly fuck. Too bad he was a cop.

"I can't."

"Why?"

"I just can't."

"You're afraid somebody is gonna hurt you?"

"Kind of."

"We're going to make you a deal. Right here on the spot. I swear this will be the last time you will ever hear about another deal like this."

Morgan tapped the table and avoided Cooper's eyes. She knew that man could make her do anything he wanted her to do if she looked at him long enough. "What kind of deal?"

"We're going to pay your daughter's tuition for her school and let you keep the handbag that you purchased with the counterfeit. Just tell us where you got the money from."

"Am I going to go to jail?"

"One hundred percent immunity."

"I got the money from a guy named Jabril."

"Who is he to you?"

"Just somebody that tricked off on me a couple of times."

"You have his number?"

"I do."

"Can I have it?"

Chapter 15

Mitch and Jen were the names of Craig's kids. Mitch was nine years old with his mother's blond hair. His adopted sister Jen was seven and had been with the family since she was three, Craig's wife sister and husband had died in a car accident and Craig and Ann became her legal guardian, now the poor girl had to deal with another tragedy in her young life. The homicide detectives had made good on their promise and had managed to arrange a visit for Craig's children, who were now in the care of their grandmother.

They sat across from him in the visitation room. Mitch bounced a rubber ball and Jen smiled. She was happy to see her father.

Craig said, "Mitch, can you put the ball down for a moment and talk to Daddy?"

The boy slung the ball against the wall, and Craig wondered how in the hell did he get the stupid ball past the jailers.

"Mitch, will you listen to me?"

"I don't wanna."

"What's wrong, son?"

"You killed Mommy."

"Who told you that?"

Mitch approached Craig and he sat down beside his sister and covered her ears with his hands. "I know you killed Mommy."

"Mitch, take your hand off my ears," Jen said.

"No, I don't want you to hear."

Craig leaned forward and said, "What don't you want her to hear?"

"I hate you. You killed my mother," Mitch said. Then he bounced out of the chair. "I wanna go."

The boy started jumping up and down screaming. "Let me out of here. I want out!"

He flung the rubber ball hard, smacking Craig's forehead.

Two jailers burst in and Mitch said, "I want out."

Craig stood and ran his fingers through Jen's hair. He planted a kiss on her forehead and said, "I love you."

"I love you too, Daddy."

Mitch slung the rubber ball at Craig again, this time missing him. "I hate you!"

Craig attempted to approach his son. One officer wedged himself between them while the other one escorted the children.

Ten minutes later, the homicide detectives entered the room.

"You've seen your children now. Are you ready to tell us what you know?"

"I need PC. I can't make it in general population."

"We're going to protect you."

"Good."

"You want to tell us about what happened to your wife?"

Craig dropped his head between his legs and sobbed. Finally he said, "It was all my fault."

●　●　●

TeTe and Butterfly had returned from a quick trip to the mall and grocery store. The doorbell rang. A courier.

TeTe signed for the package then tore into the box. Another phone. She dialed the number and recognized the voice immediately. The same voice of the kidnapper. She and

Butterfly entered the kitchen and began putting away the groceries.

"What do you want?"

"You think I'm playing?"

"What the fuck are you talking about?"

"Bitch, you knew that money was counterfeit."

"I don't know shit." TeTe then said to Butterfly, "Go upstairs and get your daddy."

"My daddy?" Butterfly grimaced.

"Go get Black, dammit!"

Butterfly sprinted upstairs, knocked on the door before entering, and found Black sprawled across the bed, asleep with his mouth open. She shook him and when he was finally awake she said, "Mommy wants you downstairs. She's putting away the groceries."

"What? You serious?"

"Yeah."

"I thought y'all were shopping."

"We just got back."

Black got up and walked downstairs into the kitchen and helped TeTe place bottled water into the fridge as he listened to her curse into the phone.

"I don't give a fuck what you do. The same way you're saying you're going to get us, you can be got, too, motherfucker!"

Black said, "What the hell is going on?"

She handed Black the phone.

"Hello."

"Motherfucker, you want to play games with me?"

"Who is this?"

"One of the clowns that kidnapped my baby girl," TeTe said.

Black terminated the call.

TeTe poured a glass of white wine. She sipped it and said, "He's saying the money was counterfeit."

"It was."

TeTe set the glass down. She took some deep breaths.

"It was high quality money."

"My baby could have gotten killed, Black! Playing around with you. Now you telling me that the money was high quality. What the fuck ever."

Black huffed. "There was no way that they were going to know the money was fake."

"You don't know that. They found out, didn't they?"

"Yeah, much later. Butterfly is home, isn't she?"

TeTe glanced at her daughter who was simply standing in the entranceway, her head turning from TeTe to Black, listening to everything. TeTe said, "Go to your room—"

"Wasn't she going to help you put the groceries up?" Black asked.

"Who the fuck asked you?" TeTe said. She sipped her wine. "My baby could have gotten killed."

Black presented her with one of the fake hundred-dollar bills.

TeTe stared at the money before ripping it up. "Is this supposed to make me feel better?"

"I was just showing you what was used."

"Did I motherfuckin' ask you what you used?"

Black sat at the kitchen table. "How was I going to come up with a million dollars?"

She sighed and said, "I guess you did what you thought was right."

"Damn right I did what I thought was right."

"Where did you get that much counterfeit from?"

"Does it matter?"

"So we keeping secrets now?"

"If I told you, you wouldn't understand."

"Tell me."

I met an FBI agent and he gave it to me."

TeTe set her wine down and said, "What the fuck do you mean you met an FBI agent? How does a person, particularly a criminal, just meet an FBI agent? It's not like you're saying that you met a teacher or met a basketball player or a fireman."

Black avoided her gaze and then said, "I was driving one day and he pulled me over and he knew everything about me. Told me about the Homeland Security investigation."

"I don't get it. So he wants to cut you a deal?"

"No. Well, he wants me to work for him, but not in the

police way. He wants to give me dope to sell that he's taken from drug dealers."

"You didn't do it, did you?"

Silence.

"You did?"

He turned and faced her. "I did. I needed the money and I needed him to make the investigation go away. When he said Homeland Security, I knew he was telling the truth because even when Lani was living, they had been investigating me."

"So you sell drugs for the Feds?"

"Well, it's just me and this agent."

"Are you out of your mind, Black?" TeTe downed her wine.

"I had no choice."

"There's always a choice. And what happens when these niggas on the street find out?"

"That's not how it works. It's not like I get him to bust drug dealers then give me the drugs. He gives me the shit and I don't know where it comes from."

"I don't trust it."

"Hey, I didn't trust it at first but I got Butterfly back home, didn't I?"

"Yes, I guess."

Black massaged TeTe's shoulder's and said, "Trust me, baby, it's going to be alright."

"I want to believe you. I wish you wouldn't do this, but you're a grown man."

"I know what I'm doing. You got to believe me."

Chapter 16

Q stopped by the studio to surprise Starr for a mid-day lunch. When he grabbed the door of the studio, he was surprised that it didn't open. Then he noticed a sign: Closed for Today. Returnon Monday. And then it listed Starr's cell phone number. When Q turned to walk away, a tall black man approached.

"Are they closed?" the man asked.

"Yeah," Q said then began walking. He stopped and turned. "You look familiar."

The black man smiled. "I used to play a little ball."

Q realized right away that this was the man in the pictures in Starr's design books. "I've heard about you?"

"Did you watch any of my games?"

"No. I heard you were trying to push up on my girl."

"What?"

"Starr is my woman."

"Are you her husband?"

"No."

"Well then, I'm sorry to tell you, she ain't your woman, partner."

Q approached Terrell. "I'm going to need you to stay away

from her."

"And if I don't?"

"You're a ballplayer, not a gangsta. So you need to stay in a ballplayer's place. Understand?"

"You don't own her."

"She's having my baby." Q didn't even blink when he told the lie.

"Your baby?"

"Yep."

"She just came to my house the other day," Terrell said.

"She told me about it. She had actually showed up to tell you to stay away, but you had company and she didn't want to make a scene."

"Like I said, you don't own her. I'll let her tell me to stay away."

He walked away and Q said, "I'm telling you to stay in your lane, bruh. Stay in your lane or you're going to get hurt."

• • •

John had found Champagne's address after three days of searching. He'd found the strip club that she worked in and followed her home one night. About one week after he had given TeTe the address, TeTe and two goons had followed her to the babysitter's house. Champagne was headed to work when a blue Toyota Avalon rammed into the back of her car. When she hopped out of the car to see the damages, two men snatched her up and tossed her into the back of the car.

Inside one of TeTe's home's in Cobb County, Champagne was hog-tied when TeTe entered the room.

TeTe said, "Do you remember me?"

Champagne nodded. "If you think I went to the po-po about Sapphire, I didn't. I swear to God, I ain't tell nobody shit."

"Why don't I believe you?"

"I swear I ain't tell nobody nothing. All I wanna do is go to work and take care of my kids. That's all I want to do. I don't want no problems."

TeTe slapped the fuck out of Champagne with a wooden

paddle. "Ho, shut the fuck up. You know why I don't believe you? Do you know why I don't believe you?"

"No."

"Because you were the one that tipped us off about your friend."

"She wasn't my friend. We just worked together at the strip club."

"Didn't I tell you to shut the fuck up?"

"I'm sorry."

TeTe sat beside her. She looked at the woman with the long weave and tiny waist and said. "You're a very good looking woman."

"Thank you."

"What's your name?"

"Champagne."

"Your real name. Your government name. I know damn well your mama didn't name you Champagne."

"She didn't. My name is Amber."

"Look, I'm going to give you an opportunity. An opportunity to save your life."

The woman smiled halfheartedly.

"First of all, I need to know if you went to the police when we killed your friend."

"No, baby, I'm from the Lou! And we don't play that shit there. Snitches get stitches. You know what I'm saying?"

"The Lou?"

"St. Louis."

"Okay."

"So what do I have to do?"

"I want to know where Rakeem and Jabril are."

"I don't know them."

One of TeTe's goons pulled out a gun and pressed it against her forehead and cocked the hammer. "If I squeeze the trigger this gun is going to take your whole block off."

"I'm sorry, but I don't know them. I swear to God I don't know them. If I knew them, I would tell you. I got kids." She turned to TeTe and saw her nostrils flare. "I swear I would tell you if I knew where they were. I don't want to die. And when you killed Sapphire, I didn't say shit. I would never tell on Black."

TeTe said, "Lower the goddamn gun." She watched Champagne's expressions. "Why are you so loyal to Black?"

"I just always liked him. He would come to the club and was always a good tipper. He always took good care of everybody. You feel me?"

"Okay. You know that's my man, right?"

"Yeah."

"Have you ever fucked him?"

"No."

TeTe slapped the fuck out of her with the paddle. "Wrong answer. Now let's try this again. Have you ever fucked him?"

"Yes, a while back."

TeTe slapped the fuck out of her again and said, "Why did you lie?"

"I don't know. I thought you would be upset."

"What else did you lie about?"

"Nothing."

"I don't know why, but I like yo lying ass," TeTe said. She stood. "I'm not going to kill you."

"Thank you."

"But you're going to have to do me a favor."

"Anything you ask."

"That's what I want to hear."

Chapter 17

Jada scrolled through her phone deleting numbers that she no longer needed. Then she came across Shantelle's number and dialed it.

"Hello."

"Hey, girl, it's Jada."

"Jada?"

"Starr's friend. You know, Trey's girl."

"Oh, hey. I didn't think I would hear from you again."

"I've been really thinking about what you told me a few weeks ago."

"Well, I thought you should know."

"Hey, do you mind telling Starr what you know?"

"I don't think Starr wants to see me."

"Listen, Trey is dead. She ain't holding no grudges. I can tell you that."

"Sure, I'll meet up with you. When?"

"I'll text you her address and we can meet over there for lunch. She and I was going to have lunch today."

"Perfect."

• • •

Starr greeted Jada and Shantelle as soon as they walked into her condo. She gave Shantelle a once-over and then hugged her.

"I'm so sorry about the past."

Starr laughed and said, "I loved Trey, but you couldn't have done anything that he didn't want to happen. He was a grown man. He made the choices he made."

Starr led Jada and Shantelle to the kitchen, and she made sandwiches and sangrias.

Jada said, "Boys will be boys. We all know that."

"We do."

Jada bit into her sandwich and said, "I want you to tell Starr what you told me."

"I didn't want to start any problems, but this was about a month before Trey was killed. Q found me."

"What do you mean found you? How did he find you?"

"Through Monte. Remember the runner that got locked up?"

"Yeah."

"Monte knew how to get in touch with me, so he found me and I met up with him at Houston's."

Jada sipped her sangria. "This shit sounds like a movie."

"Well, anyway, we were having lunch and he was asking me did I like Trey. At the time, we were having problems and I over shared what was going on in our home."

"What did you tell him?" Starr asked.

"I told him that Trey was still in love with you. And he said that I needed to make it work with him. Then I said it wasn't going to work." She looked Starr in her eyes. "You were the woman that he loved, not me. I loved Trey but when I saw that he was still in love with you, I knew that it wasn't going to work."

This made Starr feel good. She didn't know why it made her feel good, but it was great hearing this from Shantelle.

"Then he asked me about what happened in Louisiana."

"What happened?"

"Trey and I got pulled with a shitload of money and dope, and the cop took the money and let us go with the dope."

"What?"

"Yeah, the man took the money and let us go."

"Damn."

"Trey and I both were shocked and I explained this to Q. But he kept trying to get me to admit that I was lying. I would never do it, and he said to me that he could have me killed. He suggested that I help him set Trey up to get killed, or get the fuck out of town. So that's when I told Jessica about it and she said that I should just take some money."

"I thought she helped you take the money?"

"She did. She was the one with the information about the stash houses. T.J. had taken a notebook with information from Trey's mother's house."

"Oh."

"Q didn't believe that the police let Trey go."

"I think he did. I think deep down inside Q knew that Trey would never cross him."

Starr's mouth fell open.

Shantelle said, "Seriously, Q wanted Trey dead and Q is a very dangerous man. He'll kill anybody or anything that gets in his way."

Chapter 18

TeTe had Champagne selling ass, and she had seen seven clients in the past two days. She felt disgusted about selling her body, but she knew that TeTe would, in fact, kill her if she didn't do what she was told. She was indebted to TeTe for allowing her to live. She had sold her body before, at the strip club, but never to so many men in a few days. Old, wrinkled white men with tiny pink penises.

Tonight, her appointment was at eight p.m, and she was hoping that the prospective client was a talker and not someone that wanted her to do tricks. Hopefully, he wouldn't want her to twerk or use a strap-on. Or lick their hairy, disgusting, musty balls. She liked the talkers, the ones that told her about how their wives were driving them crazy.

Champagne stood in front of Room 567 at the Four Seasons hotel when she heard a black man's voice say, "Bitch, if you don't want to do what the fuck I say, you can get the fuck on." Was this a mistake? She served mostly white clients. She dialed TeTe's number just to make sure she was at the right room.

"Hello."

"I'm at the Four Seasons. What room did you say?"

"567."

"I think you must be mistaken. These are black people."

"Sweetheart, I don't make mistakes."

"Oh." She terminated the call and tapped on the door again. The man was still fussing.

"You don't know how to fuck," he said, "and I'm about to show you exactly what I want."

The man opened the door. He introduced himself as Gerald and said that his girlfriend's name was April.

Gerald was tall with a smooth and dark tone. He looked to be about thirty-four. He was wearing expensive Gucci sneakers and a BulgariEgron watch. A hustler for sure.

April was a beautiful, light-skin woman with short curly hair. Her body was below average. Skinny legs, a small ass, and narrow hips. She was barefoot.

Champagne made her way through the door and Gerald closed it. She wore a fake smile.

Gerald eyed her thighs and licked his lips like he was a hungry coyote, and she was a piece of fresh carcass. "Have a seat."

Champagne took a seat in a chair that was in front of the desk, in the corner next to the window. The curtain was pulled back and she could see the Atlanta skyline.

Gerald said, "Do you want something to drink? We got Hennessy. Cîroc. And she has wine or we can order you something to drink."

"Henny on the rocks."

Gerald poured her a glass of Hennessy. Champagne sipped the liquor until Gerald pulled up a chair beside her and said, "You are so fucking curvy." And he smiled as though April were not in the room.

Champagne relaxed, removed her jacket and stood at the window looking out in the night sky. She thought about her kids. She hadn't seen them in days. TeTe had her working all day. Every day. She felt more comfortable with Gerald and April. She had sucked enough pink penises for the last few weeks, and in a way, she was relieved that Gerald and April were black. But Gerald's perverted grin made her nervous.

Gerald held a glass.

She felt his gaze on her ass. She turned and met his eyes.

"You want to know why you're here?"

She smiled, revealing her dimples. Trying to keep a positive attitude. "Girl on girl?"

"Not at all." Gerald set the wine glass down. His pants bulging. She had envisioned a tiny snake. But he was packing, that's for damn sure. She could tell that the head of it was huge. She knew that most skinny men had huge dicks.

"A threesome?"

"No."

She turned to April, who was still standing there with that phony smile plastered on her face. Revealing beautiful, perfect teeth. "Oh, and I thought I was going to get to taste Ms. April. She's a cutie." She winked.

"Not tonight."

"She shrugged and said, "I'm confused."

Gerald approached her and she set her drink down on the desk. Gerald set his glass of wine down as well. Then he pulled her closer and gripped a handful of ass.

"So you're going to fuck me in front of your woman?"

Dumb-ass April was still looking on. She was frowning now.

Champagne said, "I don't think April is cool with this."

"I don't give a fuck about what April is cool with. I'm paying you."

"Okay, I don't understand what you want."

"Madam didn't tell you?"

Gerald had been a client of TeTe's for six years and he had always referred to her as Madam.

"She didn't tell me anything."

His hand massaged her left ass cheek. "Take off your clothes."

Champagne removed her shoes and her dress, stripping down to a bright yellow G-string that contrasted with her dark skin wonderfully.

Gerald dropped his pants and was now in a pair of black boxer briefs.

April was leaving in a hurry but Gerald chased her down and blocked the door. He shoved her to the floor and said, "Where the fuck do you think you're going?"

Tears rolled down her cheek. "I can't believe you're going to do this to me."

Champagne grabbed her liquor and watched the two of them.

"Sit your ass right there on the flo."

"What is going on?" Champagne asked.

"I want you to teach this bitch how to suck dick. Teach her how to please her man." Gerald's face turned lethal and he turned to April and said, "Stay yo ass on the flo."

April tried to get up. Gerald grabbed his pants that were crumpled on the floor, removed a gun and cocked it. "Bitch, if you get up I'll blow a hole in yo scrawny-ass back."

"What the hell is going on, Gerald? I ain't ask to be involved in all this bullshit," Champagne said.

Gerald turned to her with a grimace on his face. "I paid Madam, and you're here to do what the fuck I say."

"I don't like this."

Gerald pointed the gun at Champagne. "Who gives a damn what you like? Bring your ass here. Get on your knees right motherfuckin' now and suck my dick."

April had her head between her legs and was crying like hell when she heard Gerald yell her name. "What?" she answered but didn't look up."

"I want you to watch this."

Champagne slurped his dick.

April said, "Gerald, why are you doing this to me?"

Gerald cocked the hammer of the gun, his dick still in Champagne's mouth. He aimed the gun at her. "Watch and learn."

April looked at her man, the man she'd been with for eight years, getting pleasured by another woman. She was dying inside. She detested this but knew that if she made Gerald mad enough, she would surely pay. Five minutes into the head, Gerald's body went into convulsions and he came inside Champagne's mouth. Gerald dropped the gun and April dropped her head between her legs, whining like a toddler.

Chapter 19

"Can I talk to you for a moment?" Terrell asked Starr. He had startled her. She was organizing her showroom and didn't see him come in. His stare was cold.

"What's wrong?"

"Do you have a moment?"

She led him to the office then offered him a seat. She sat down and his eyes were still very much on her. He wasn't cracking a smile. There was an awkward silence between the two of them and finally he said, "So you're pregnant?"

"What?"

"Are you pregnant?"

"Where did you get that from?" She seriously was trying to figure it out. How in the hell did he know that? They had no friends in common.

"I'm going to ask you again. Are you pregnant?"

"Wait a goddamn minute. You are not my father."

"I just asked you a question."

"We are not together."

"So it's true; you're pregnant by that thug-ass boyfriend?"

"I'm not pregnant by him."

"That's not what he said."

"You saw him?"

He sighed and then said, "I came by here the other day and he was here."

"When?"

"I decided to drop by one day because I didn't like the way you were looking at me when you came to my house."

"When did you come by? Brooke never told me."

"Nobody was here. In fact, you were closed. But he was leaving or maybe he thought you were open. He told me that I needed to stay the hell away from you and you were having his baby."

"That's not true."

Terrell ran his fingers through his hair. "You know, I really don't get you."

"What is there to get?"

"You show up at my home, appear to be mad that I've moved on, and yet you are still seeing this guy. Why did you even show up at my house?"

"I know it sounds crazy."

"It is crazy."

Starr stood and locked eyes with him. His eyes were very sad. She said, "I have something to tell you."

"What?"

"I am pregnant."

"You just said you weren't pregnant."

"I never said I wasn't pregnant. I said I wasn't pregnant by him."

"What the fuck? How many motherfuckers are you screwing? Do I need to get checked for an STD?"

She slapped the fuck out of him.

He held his jaw. "What the hell did you hit me for?"

"Because you just basically called me a ho."

"Well—"

"I'm pregnant by you. And I came to your house to tell you that."

"What!"

She sat down again. "I came by your house to tell you that, but when I saw that you were happy with J-Ho, I didn't want to tell you. I couldn't."

"Are you fuckin serious?"

"Yes."

"But Q is your boyfriend, right?"

"It's complicated."

"You told him you're pregnant by me?"

"I told him everything." She turned to avoid his gaze. "I thought he was the father."

Terrell smiled. "You have no idea how this makes me feel."

Starr said, "This is what I wanted to talk to you about."

"About killing my baby?"

"It's not a baby."

"Depends on who you ask." His smile turned into a frown. "So you came to tell me that you were pregnant and that you're having an abortion?"

"I don't know what I'm going to do."

He looked at her with pleading eyes and said, "I realize that you don't want me. I realize that we can never probably be together, but I want this baby. I really want the baby."

"I understand, but this is not what I planned for my life. I never planned to be somebody's baby mother. I wanted the man that I have a child with to be the man that I kept for life."

"Starr, you have to have this baby. You have to."

Starr looked at him with sad eyes. She could see the pain in his face. "I love somebody else."

• • •

Black met Agent Daniels at an abandoned warehouse on an off-road near Buford Highway, and from there you could easily see Mercy Care North Medical Clinic. Big trucks and cars of all sorts zoomed past with aggravating noises and, sometimes, unpleasant smells.

Black sat on the hood of the car gazing at the sky when Daniels approached, dressed all in black. He frowned at Black and said, "I told you to drive a truck. I've got 200 pounds of weed on me. What the fuck are you doing? No way this shit is going to fit in the car."

"We need to talk."

"About what?"

Black said, "Motherfucker, you gave me counterfeit money." He had pretended to know this when he'd discussed it with TeTe, but he wouldn't have known if she hadn't told him.

"Are you serious, Black? You wanna talk about me giving you counterfeit money now? I saved your ass. I recovered your money that you could have lost from Bird, and now the little girl is home safe and this is what you want to talk to me about? You should be more grateful."

"Why didn't you tell me? I had to fake like I already knew when my woman broke the news to me."

"The counterfeit was A-1, top of the line."

"You should have told me. You should have kept it one hundred with me, man."

"Is the girl home safe?"

"You know she is."

"Then what the hell is the matter with you? I have a shitload of weed that I need you to get rid of."

Black bounced from the hood of his car and stepped behind it. He pissed for three minutes straight. Shook his dick off and slowly made his way back to face Daniels. "I'm not doing shit with you, bruh. That's the kind of shit I don't like. I mean, you're right, we got Butterfly back, but she could have gotten killed."

"She could have, but she didn't."

"That's not the point."

"What's the point?"

"You didn't tell me. It wasn't your decision to make for me and my woman."

"You made at least three hundred thousand dollars with me in the last month."

"Money ain't everything."

"You and I both know it's the only thing. Why in the hell do you think I'm doing this? I tried to be one of the good guys. I wanted to be an honorable cop, but I just got sick and tired of locking up motherfuckers that had way more than I have."

"And that's your reason for becoming a rogue FBI agent?"

"What do you want, Black. I'll give you a bigger percentage. I need you and you need me."

Black stared with a confused expression. "Give me one reason I need you."

"You need me to stay out of jail."

"Whatever."

"Black, don't cross me. You don't want to fuck me."

"Fuck you." Black got in the car and drove away.

Chapter 20

Jada received a call from an attorney named Thomas Rawls at 3:34 p.m. "What do you want to see me for?"

"It's about a client of mine."

"What client?"

"Dr. Craig Matthews."

"Don't call me no goddamn more."

"Listen, you'll want to talk to me. I have information that might be beneficial to you. Can you come down to my office to see me?"

That sounded convincing, so twenty-five minutes later, Jada strolled into the law firm of Thomas Rawls. It was 6:30. The secretary had gone for the day. Mr. Rawls greeted her.

Thomas Rawls was a tall white man with an oval face, sleepy eyes, and thin lips. He was dressed in an Armani suit. He invited Jada to his office. When she was seated, she caught Rawls stealing a peek at her chest. Her evil look made him refocus.

He said, "I'm sorry."

"Why am I here?"

"Dr. Matthews asked me to contact you."

"He didn't have my number."

"I've got one of the best private eye's in the city."

"Why am I here?"

"There was a murder. Anne Matthews."

"I don't know shit about him killing his wife."

Rawls laughed before looking at Jada's full and succulent lips. Briefly, he imagined those lips on his little white dick. "Jada...Miss Simone."

"Yes."

"There was a girl named Imani James

died on the operating table in Dr. Matthews' office."

Jada frowned and said, "Yeah, that was the bitch that he had lied about and said Shamari made him stuff her tits with drugs. And said Shamari made him traffic drugs."

Rawls raised his eyebrows. "Well, now he wants to make it right."

"How?"

"He's going to recant his statement that he made about Shamari."

"And what good is that going to do him? Seriously, he has life already."

"He can get a new trial."

"He pled guilty."

"He can claim coercion, saying he was not put on notice of the possibility of life in prison, and also say that his attorney was ineffective."

"And he can get his sentence overturned?" Jada's lips were dry, so she licked them.

Rawls' dick came alive and he stared at her mouth.

"Could you stop that, please?"

"Excuse me?"

"Staring at me in a creepy-ass way."

"I'm very sorry. Rarely do I get to see someone as beautiful as you are."

"Thanks, but no more creepy looks."

He smiled.

"I don't understand. Why would he do this? What's in this for him?"

"He needs you to pay his legal fees."

"What the fuck? Are you serious?"

"Yes, well, unless you have been living under a rock, you know that he is facing a murder-for-hire charge."

"Yeah, I heard about it." Jada stood and paced. She didn't know how she would feel about paying for this man's legal fees. As far as she was concerned, he was the devil. She flipped her hair over her shoulder, her electric blue dress glued to her ass, and Rawls saw her thong print.

"How much are the legal fees?"

"I don't know."

"He's pleading guilty, I presume?"

"Yes."

"So if he's pleading guilty, I know his bitch-ass is snitching. So why do he need money for a lawyer?"

"It's not that simple. Dr. Matthews is fighting for his life. He's trying not to get the death penalty."

"You struck a deal?"

"We did, but it's up to the judge."

"And it will also be up to a judge if Shamari can get out?"

"I don't know the circumstances in your boyfriend's case, but if Dr. Matthews recants the statement, there is a chance that he gets a new trial."

Jada would do anything for Shamari, but damn, she didn't want to help Craig at all. She would have to think about this. "I'll call you."

"I need to know in one week."

Chapter 21

Starr wanted to strip down butt naked when she smelled the Nuits de Noho Bond No. 9 candle. But she wasn't there for that. She marched right by him without speaking. He offered her a seat.

"I'll stand."

"You know, Q, you really need to fuckin grow up."

He shrugged his shoulders. And she had to admit that he was looking cute in navy blue boxer briefs and nothing else.

"What are you talking about?"

"I'm talking about how you ran down on Terrell."

Q laughed and tried to embrace Starr but she shoved him.

"Why are you worried about that lame-ass dude?" He sat and propped his feet on the coffee table. Starr sat in an armchair across from him.

"So you're here to curse me out? Go ahead, curse me the fuck out, Starr. I told the lame motherfucker that you were pregnant. I want to be with you. He doesn't deserve you."

"Why did you tell him I was having your baby?"

Q rubbed his goatee. "I don't see what the fuck is the big deal. I told you I think you should have the baby and I'll take care of it. He doesn't need to know that it's his."

"I told him."

"Why did you tell him?"

"He asked me was I pregnant and I told him. He deserves to know."

Q sighed and threw his hands up in disgust. "Now we're in a fucked-up position. I really wanted to raise this baby."

"You have one in Houston."

"That's fucked up, Starr, that you would say something like that."

She covered her face. "I don't know what I'm going to do."

"Have the child. I support you, baby!"

"Q, you can't be serious. Do you think I really want to be with you? Do you think I should be with you? I don't even know who the fuck you are."

"And what is that supposed to mean?"

"You wanted to kill the love of my life."

He narrowed his eyes. "We're back on this shit again?"

"What shit?"

"Starr, I made a mistake. I thought Trey was going to give us all up. So I thought I had to knock him off. But I didn't kill Trey."

"But you wanted to. I don't know if I can live with that."

"Bottom line, Trey is dead and I'm not the one that killed him."

"I know."

"Why you keep bringing it up?"

She looked at him with serious eyes. "I know you believed him when he said that the police took the money."

The candle went out. He lit another one. This time it was High Line Bond No. 9. "What the fuck is that supposed to mean?"

"Stop yelling."

"I'm sorry, babe, but I don't like that you're accusing me of something that I didn't do. I didn't kill Trey, and you know it."

"But you knew Trey was telling the truth when he told you that he had gotten pulled and the cops took the money and let him go. You knew Trey didn't tell on you. What is the real reason you wanted to kill him?"

Q avoided her eyes. "Where are you getting all this from?"

"Does it matter?"

"That Shantelle bitch is putting this in your head."

"Why did you want to kill Trey?"

"You wouldn't understand."

She rushed up to him and pounded his chest. "I hate you."

He restrained her and said, "I did want him dead. I was jealous of what he had. I'd always wanted you and I needed him out of the way. He would come down to Houston and he would show off pictures of you and him vacationing on some island. And you giving him surprise birthday parties. Him with your family. I wanted that. I'm sorry, but I thought with him out of the way, I could be with you. I love you, Starr. I always have loved you, and I want to take care of this baby. Our baby."

Starr said, "Motherfucker, get your hands off me! Get away from me right now."

Q released her and Starr ran out of the house.

Chapter 22

Jada answered the door wearing some cut-off booty shorts and a wife-beater.

Black could see her nipple print, and when she turned to lead him into the living room, he could see her ass cheeks peeking out. "Damn, girl."

"Black, don't start with me. Matter of fact, let me cover myself up. Damn. All you men think about is getting some ass."

"Honestly, that slipped, but damn you fine."

"I asked you not to start."

He grinned.

She dipped into the bedroom and came back out wearing a sweat suit.

"I can't believe you did that."

"Yesterday, I had this creepy-ass lawyer looking at me like I was a piece of steak or something."

"Hey, girl, I'm hungry. What you got in here to eat? Any more of your mama's mac and cheese?"

"No."

"Then what?"

"There is some cold Papa John's pizza in the fridge."

"Pizza?" He made a sad face. "Damn these new school women. Don't nobody cook no more?"

"Black, I didn't call you over here to raid my fridge. I have a serious issue."

"What's going on?"

"Remember the doctor that lied on Shamari? That got him in all the bullshit?"

"Yeah?"

"He killed his wife and now he wants to help Shamari."

"Help him out? How? Why?"

"He is going to take back his statement, say that he was coerced. According to the lawyer, he can get back in court."

Black stood. "I don't get it. Why would he do that?"

"He wants us to pay his legal fees."

"What the fuck you mean us?"

"Nigga, you and Shamari were partners. You need to help out, too."

"I'll do whatever I can to help Shamari; you know that, but I need to make sure this ain't no scam. You feel me?" Black walked to the kitchen, grabbed the Papa John's box, and warmed the pizza up. He returned munching on a slice.

"What happened to all the new-school-women talk?"

"I'm hungry and that's all yo ass got in here."

"So you think we should do this?"

"Let me talk to Joey Turch."

"Please talk to him."

"How much money are we talking about paying for this dude?"

"A hundred to a hundred and fifty thousand."

"And how much do you have?"

"I have the money, but I thought since you and Mari were partners, you would contribute."

"And I will. Can I talk to my attorney first?"

• • •

Shantelle was excited about her new pink Nike running shoes, which matched her new workout pink leggings with black zebra stripes. She'd taken two selfies—one from the back since it was hump day. She had worked really hard to grow her glutes, so why not show them off? Now, it was time for a morning run.

She stepped outside her townhome then bent down to tie her laces up extra tight. That's when she felt the cold steel on the side of her neck.

"Stand up now, bitch, and this is what we are going to do," the man said. He snatched her up by the hair.

"Don't hurt me."

"This is what you're going to do. You're going to go inside and disarm the alarm."

"There ain't no alarm." She fumbled with the key before opening the door.

When they were inside, he said, "Okay, there is no silent alarm?"

"No. I swear to God."

She finally saw him. Tall black man wearing a ski mask. She saw only his eyes. "What do you want from me?" Her voice was louder now. "I don't have money but I have jewelry. Valuable jewelry and lots of shoes and handbags. You can have it all. Just don't hurt me."

"You know what, Shantelle..."

"You know me?"

"You talk too fuckin' much. It didn't have to come down to this. You could have left town like I asked you to do. But, no, you wanted to stay around here and run your goddamn mouth. Now you're going to have to pay, bitch." He revealed the gun and she saw the silencer.

She said, "Q?" As he began pointing the gun, she gestured towards a small camera sitting on the top of the bookcase.

When he spotted the camera, he saw a flashing blue light. He struck out running toward the door and it slowed him only for a half second. She trailed him and saw him sprint up a hill and jump into a winter-green Jeep Cherokee.

The fake security camera had actually come in handy. Her leggings were soaked. She laughed. She'd actually pissed in her pants. But it could have been much worse and she saw the urine run down her legs into her new Nikes.

Chapter 23

Black entered Nana's house and hugged his two children, Man-Man and Tierany.

Tierany said to Black, "Daddy, I want you to come to my race on Saturday."

"What race?"

"I'm running in my first five k."

"Of course I'll be there. Where is it?"

"I'll text you the time and place."

Black kissed his daughter on the forehead then asked the kids to excuse him and Nana. After they were gone, Black said, "How long they been here?"

"They been here since you told them to come over here."

"Good."

"Boy, what the hell is going on?"

"Nothing."

"I know when your black ass is lying."

Black looked at his grandma. Her hands rested on her hips.

"Now, tell me why all of a sudden you call me and tell me that your kids and child's mother need to stay with me?"

"A friend of mine murdered three people a few months ago."

"I heard, and they locked your ass up for it. But then let you go."

"Right."

"I'm not understanding."

"Well, you know that police are after my ass, and the last time they caught up with me, it was because my baby mama told on me."

"Because you used her car in the murder. What the hell was she supposed to do?"

"I get that." Black avoided Nana's eyes. He didn't like lying to her but he had to tell her something. He couldn't let her know that killers had threatened to kill his kids. "And I know that we haven't heard the last of those cops."

"You believe they are going to bring up the charges again?"

"That's exactly what I think and I think they are going to use my baby mama to get me." Black knew this didn't make a lot of sense, but he didn't think Nana would dig too much deeper.

"That's a damn lie and you know it, Tyrann. I know yo ass is up to no good but if staying here is going to keep them babies safe, they can stay here as long as they want."

Black leaned forward and kissed Nana. "Thanks."

"Before you leave, a courier delivered a package for you."

"What kind?"

"I don't know. I didn't open it." Nana disappeared into the bedroom and came back with a box.

Black tore into it.

A cell phone. The Detroit boys knew exactly where his kids were. He had to get them out of there in a hurry.

• • •

As soon as Asia entered Nana's house, Black pulled her aside and led her to his childhood bedroom and slammed the door before locking it. She looked concerned. He noticed she had passion marks on her neck. "You've been seeing someone?"

"What?"

"You have a new man?"

"Black, what the fuck is this all about? You worried about

who I'm fucking? All the bitches you've fucked over the years. I know damn well you ain't worried about what I'm doing."

He stared at Asia. He had never before thought that she was seeing someone. He didn't want to think about it. Although he hadn't been with her for years, he loved her and he thought she would always belong to him in some capacity.

He stared at the passion marks, thinking she had shared her body with another man. Not that he was so foolish as to believe that he was the only man that she'd ever been with, but there was never any evidence to suggest otherwise. Now there was rock-solid evidence on her neck.

"Black, when are you going to tell us what the fuck is going on? And don't give me that shit about you think the police is going to pick me up and use me to try to get more evidence on that triple murder case."

"Okay, I'm gonna tell you what's going on."

"Tell me."

"Does he make you happy?"

"Huh? What is this about? Why are you drilling me about who I'm fucking?"

"First, tell me that he makes you happy?"

She sighed. "God, you make me sick."

"Answer the question?"

"I'm happy."

Black gave her a fake smile and said, "Well, then I'm happy for you. But don't let no motherfucker put their hands on my kids."

"He hasn't even met the kids yet."

"Good. I don't want him to meet them until I meet him."

"Now can you tell me what the fuck is going on?"

"Promise not to tell Nana?"

"She ain't hardly stupid."

"I know she ain't stupid; I learned all my game from her. Nana used to be the candy lady and she sold loose cigarettes in the hood. Don't let the bible fool you."

"Black, you're getting off the subject. What the fuck are we doing over here?"

"Some niggas are after me, and they are going to try to get at me in any way they can."

"So you think they are going to try to get us? Why do you think this?"

"They know where you live."

"I see you didn't learn from the time they kidnapped Man-Man. What the fuck!" She paced and said, "I don't know if I can stay here too long; I just got into this new relationship and how in the hell am I going to explain to my man that I'm staying with my baby daddy's grandmother? I know that shit ain't gone fly."

"I gotta get y'all out of here anyway. They know where Nana lives now."

"What?"

"How do you know this?"

"Just know that I know for sure."

Asia sat down on the bed and Black tried to massage her shoulders. She slapped his hands and said, "I ain't in the mood for your shit."

He sat down beside her.

Asia said, "There ain't no way Nana is going to be safe here."

"I know."

"So what are you going to do?"

"She's always talking about she wants to see her sister in Mississippi before she dies. I'm gonna just get my sister to take her."

"When?"

"Tomorrow."

"So we are leaving tomorrow? Where will we go? You know I don't get along with my mama and won't stay there."

"I'll find somewhere for you to go. But like I said, I don't want no man around my kids."

"Fuck you, Black."

Chapter 24

Shantelle telephoned Jada and said that she needed to see her and Starr right away. They met at RA Sushi bar. Jada and Shantelle had Mojitos and Starr had a virgin daiquiri.

Starr kept staring at Shantelle and she wondered what her story was. She had never had a chance to talk to her, but she seemed like a very nice girl. Not the kind of girl that grew up in the hood like Jada and herself, but Starr did know that all girls wanted bad boys at some point in their life. She couldn't imagine this woman being a drug mule, and she didn't want to think that she had been with Trey. She wanted to hate Shantelle but she couldn't. She couldn't blame her for fuckin her man.

"What did you want that you didn't want to talk over the phone about?" Jada asked.

"Q tried to kill me."

"What?" Starr's face displayed a look of surprise.

Shantelle cleared her throat. "He broke into my house, wearing a ski mask. He was going to kill me."

Jada looked confused. "How do you know it was him?"

"He said I talked too much and that he was going to make me pay. He pulled a gun out on me." She looked at Starr. "I recognized his voice."

"What? No way."

"I wish I was lying, but he said that he was going to make me pay."

Jada sipped her drink then said, "Why didn't he shoot? Not that I wanted him to shoot."

"He didn't shoot because I pointed at a fake camera that sat on my bookcase. When he spotted it, he took off running."

"What?" Jada seemed to be picturing the event.

"Q was going to kill me," Shantelle said.

Jada looked at Starr and said, "I believe her. Q is not a good guy. That nigga ain't shit."

"I saw him the other day and he was mad that I had told Terrell I'm pregnant. He had gone and told him that he had me pregnant." Starr sipped her drink.

"Q admitted that he had wanted Trey dead, and he admitted that he knew Trey was telling the truth about getting stopped and getting the money taken without arrest."

"He knew Trey was telling the truth?" Jada was shaking her head.

"Okay, he wanted Trey dead. Why? It doesn't make sense. Trey was one of his top customers. Why in the hell would he want Trey dead?" Shantelle said.

Starr said, "He claimed he wanted him dead because he wanted to be with me. He wanted him out of the way."

Jada pointed at Starr. "That motherfucker is crazy. I don't give a fuck how much you love him, get away from him."

Shantelle said, "Jada is right."

* * *

Black entered TeTe's house with the box in his hand that he had brought from Nana's house.

TeTe's eyes expanded. She recognized the package design. She had also received the same type of throwaway phone. "Where the hell did you get that from?"

"They sent it to my Nana."

"They know where she lives? You have got to get her the fuck out of there."

"I know what I got to do. I let her know that her sister in Mississippi was sick and I'm arranging for her to go to Mississippi."

"She's not sick?"

"She's ninety. I know damn well she has some kind of ailment."

TeTe laughed and said, "So what's the plan?"

"I don't know what the plan is. All I know is that we gotta get her the hell out of there. Gotta get somewhere for my kids to go."

"I know." TeTe made her way into the kitchen and poured a glass of gin and cranberry juice. She sat at the bar and sipped her drink.

"Did your bullshit PI ever find out anything?"

"No."

"We need him to find out something on them."

"What about that bitch? You know the one that we should have killed. Do you think she knows anything?" TeTe asked.

"She doesn't know them."

"And you believe her?"

"I do but I will track her down and ask her."

TeTe said, "Don't worry about her." There was no way she could be tracked down. Champagne was somewhere with a $9,000 per night client. TeTe downed her drink and poured some more. "Don't stress it, baby."

"Where is Butterfly?"

"She's with my sister. I let her hold one of the cars."

"Okay."

TeTe stood behind Black and massaged his shoulders. He tilted his head backward, making eye contact, and said, "Damn, that feels good."

She kissed him and he tasted liquor. He gripped her ass. Commando, he thought. His dick jumped and she gripped it through his pants.

Black froze-up and looked ahead again. "Are you sure Butterfly is not here? I think I heard something."

"Relax. I'm sure." She peeled out of her pants. Butt naked, just as he'd imagined. His dick was throbbing at the site of her pussy lips hanging.

She dropped to her knees, her hand massaging his rock-solid manhood through his jeans. He kicked off his shoes, removed his jeans then stepped out of his blue boxer briefs. Her hand stroked the head of his dick. She took him deep inside her wet mouth.

Black heard a sound again and he stopped her. "I know I'm not crazy, babe. There is someone here." He tried to grab his pants and she stopped him.

Eli appeared.

"What the fuck is he doing here?"

"He's going to watch."

"What?"

"You had your threesome, didn't you? With Sapphire?"

Black shrugged. "I didn't ask for that."

Eli sat on the edge of the bed and he watched as TeTe took Black deep inside her throat.

Black felt uneasy about Eli sitting a few feet away, now with his boxers were down by his ankles, stroking his little dick. When Black caught that, he said, "Hey, what the fuck is he doing? I don't want to see him."

TeTe backed him into the bed and said, "Don't look at him. Why are you looking in that direction in the first place?"

Black and TeTe kissed before she hopped up on top and straddled him. Eli was now pacing, and this made Black nervous. TeTe signaled for Eli to come closer, and so he did, his dick still swinging wildly. She took Eli in her mouth.

Black slid from underneath her. TeTe was now situated on her hands and knees, and Black entered her from behind and she sucked Eli off.

Black fucked her with aggression and passion. He never figured that TeTe was normal, but he knew that after today, he could never look at her the same.

He breathed heavily as he made eye contact with Eli, who had his manhood down her throat.

Eli sat on the bed and TeTe licked his balls.

Black slapped her ass hard and kept fucking her. She turned to face Black and said, "Switch up with Eli and do me bad, Daddy."

Eli changed positions with Black. Eli entered her and

humped until his thighs smacked her ass cheeks.

TeTe looked up at Black and said, "Do me bad, daddy."

"What?"

"Rub your dick on my face."

"What the fuck?"

She took hold of his dick and rubbed it across her face. The sounds of Eli's thighs smacking her cheeks grew louder. TeTe was still slapping Black's penis across her face.

Eli withdrew and TeTe turned and said, "What are you doing?"

He sat on the edge of the bed and said, "I can't do this."

TeTe lay on the bed facedown and said to Black, "Fuck me, daddy! Fuck me. This whack motherfucker can't fuck anyhow...never could."

Black moved behind TeTe and started working her from behind. He yanked her hair.

Eli was heading toward the door and TeTe said, "Motherfucker, don't you leave! Stay here and watch a real man fuck me like you never could."

Eli ignored her and Black kept pounding until she climaxed multiple times.

Eli had seen enough. He returned minutes later with a scowl. TeTe was on her back when she spotted Eli suddenly charging Black with a metal object. She thrust Black onto the floor and yelled, "He has a knife!"

Black sprang to his feet and was face to face with Eli. TeTe scrambled to the other side of the bed and removed her little pink .380 and aimed it. "Put the damn knife down, motherfucker!"

Eli began to cry and said, "Why did you do me like this? You know I loved you and you still want to fuck another man."

TeTe said, "Put the damn knife down, motherfucker."

"I love you, TeTe."

"I said put the knife down, or I'm going to have to blast your ass."

"You let this motherfucker come in between us."

TeTe cocked the hammer on the gun.

"I know I fucked up. I know I shouldn't have been cheating. But you moved on too quickly."

"Eli, when I'm done counting to ten, that fucking knife better be on the damn floor."

"Do what you gotta do."

"I don't wanna kill you."

Eli lunged toward Black with the knife, and TeTe fired six shots into Eli's upper body. He crashed to the bed, his chest ripped open, and gasped slowly before taking his last breath.

Black scrambled to put on his clothes. When he was dressed he simply said, "What the fuck? This is the craziest shit I've ever been a part of."

TeTe grabbed her phone from the dresser and called John. He would have to clean up the place and get rid of the body.

Chapter 25

It was three in the morning when Starr opened the door for Q. He stepped inside and walked past her. She was still half asleep, her hands resting on her hips, and a bonnet on her head. She wore a white bathrobe.

"So what's going on?" She glanced at her clock. "Why so late?"

"I needed to see you."

"About what?"

His eyes blinked rapidly. "Can I have a seat?"

"There is no need for us to sit down. I have to get some sleep, so whatever you need to tell me, please tell me now. I have to take T.J. to school in the morning. So what's on your mind, man?"

"I've been thinking about us."

"Us?"

"I don't want to lose you."

"Lose me? I don't even know who the fuck you are now."

"What is that supposed to mean?"

"Your past is going to catch up with you sooner or later."

"If you want me to stop hustling, I will. I got one more shipment coming in and after that, I'm done. It will be me, you, T.J., and the baby." His eyes looked sincere.

"It can never be just us."

"Why not?"

"Q, you have other obligations. Other children. You're telling me that you're going to just cut them off?"

"You know what I mean."

"I don't even know you."

"I want to marry you, Starr." He grabbed her hand and smiled. "We can buy a big house out in Cobb County. I'll buy two houses next to each other. One for me and you and the kids, and the other for your parents. So you can have your support system right next to you."

"Oh my God. Do you think I'm that stupid? You just say you want to marry me and I'll forget that you tried to murder my best friend?"

"Lani was your best friend."

"You know what I mean."

"I did want to kill Trey, but I've apologized for that."

"Shhh. T.J. is asleep. I don't want him to ever hear you say that."

"My bad." He inched toward her. "Is there a chance?"

"No."

"Why?"

"I'm convinced you're a sociopath."

"I didn't kill anyone."

"You tried, though."

"I never tried to kill Trey."

"What about Shantelle?"

Silence.

T.J. burst out of the room wearing Star Wars pajamas. When he spotted Q, he ran up to him and hugged him.

"How are you doing, champ?"

"When are you going to take me to another game?"

"Golden State is coming next week. We'll go to that one!"

"Steph Curry!"

"Yes." He looked at a clearly pissed-off Starr and said, "Well, only if your mom don't hate on us."

T.J. turned to Starr and said, "Can I go to the game with Uncle Q?"

"We'll see, T.J."

T.J. said, "Mom is a hater." Then he displayed a sad face.

Starr said, "I'll take you to the game, but right now go get some rest for school in the morning."

T.J. smiled and said, "Bye, uncle."

After T.J. disappeared, Starr said, "You need to be going, too."

"I'll leave if you tell me whether there is a chance for us?"

"No chance. We're done. You're crazy and don't come back here again."

• • •

Black called Daniels and met up with him at the old warehouse just off Buford Highway again. Daniels was dressed in grass-stained jeans and a black thermal shirt that was torn at the elbows. His face was serious and he said, "Make it fast. I've had a bad night."

"What happened to you?" Black said.

"Short version of the story: We were chasing some bank robbers through the woods."

"I see."

"I didn't expect to hear from you again."

"I need your help."

He laughed. "My help?"

"Seriously."

"Fuck you, dude! Isn't that what you told me? I ask you to help me and you didn't. I'm not letting myself be used by you."

Black said calmly, "Man, you need me and I need you. I'll help you sell as much dope as you need me to sell. Just look out for me."

"What do you want?"

"My friend Shamari...I think I told you about him."

"In the Atlanta Pen?"

"Yeah, him."

"What about him?"

"Did you hear about the doctor that killed his wife? It's been all over the news."

"Dr. Matthews."

"Yeah, he is one of the reasons my friend is behind bars. He lied on my friend, said he forced him to traffic dope. Forced him to stuff this chick's titties with dope. Shamari pled guilty and now Matthews is recanting his statement."

"Okay, well maybe your friend can get a new trial."

"That's what the doctor is saying he's gonna do, but he wants us to come up with his attorney fees."

"And then he'll take his statement back?"

"Yeah."

"I hope you don't want me to help you with that."

"No, I just need you to make sure he is doing what he says he is going to do."

"This is important to you."

"This is my brother I'm talking about."

"I got a shitload of coke I need you to move. You helping, right?"

"Yes. I'll do whatever you need me to do, bruh."

"His charges are with the state?"

"But, you're the Feds, bruh. Pull some strings. Get my boy out. You feel me?"

"I'll do what I can."

"One more thing."

"I'm going to give you the info on the kidnappers. The niggas that kidnapped the little girl. I want you to drum up a charge on them or something. I need them off the street."

Daniels eyebrows raised. "Black, you're giving up names?"

"I ain't got no choice. I can't let my family get hurt."

"Can you tell me what's going on? Why are they after you?"

"Their brother Shakur got murdered and they think I had something to do with it."

"Did you?"

"No," Black lied.

"What are their names?"

"Jabril and Rakeem Campbell."

"I'll get somebody to trail them. Plant some guns on them and take them in. Get their bonds denied."

"Preciate you, man."

Chapter 26

Brooke and DeMontre made out on the hood of her car in front of DeMontre's house. She had told her parents that she was going to spend the night with her friend Bethany. And she would be there by morning before Bethany's mother got off. Her mother was a nurse that worked night shift while Brooke was somewhere making out with DeMontre. Bethany was with her boyfriend. A college dude.

DeMontre's hand cuffed her perky little ass and he tongue-kissed her neck.

"Don't bite me."

"It's called marking your territory."

"Please don't do it. Last time my dad was asking all kinds of questions."

"I wanna meet yo pops."

"No."

"Why not?"

"He won't like you."

DeMontre made a sad face. "Why don't you think he'll like me? Is it because I'm from the hood?"

"No. He don't like any of the boys that I date."

"Even that last cornball?"

"He didn't like him either."

"But you said he let him come over."

"That's because he attends the same church as us."

"I don't go to church."

"I know."

She felt his hairy little chest. She leaned closer and rested her head on his chest. The scent of his armpits turned her on.

"I love you."

"I love you too and I want to be with you. I don't give a damn what my pops say, I'm going to be with you."

He looked away. "I wish that was true."

"You think I'm lying?"

"Of course. Next year you'll go away to some big-time college and forget all about me."

"I'm staying in Atlanta."

"You would do that for me?"

"Anything for you."

"Anything?"

"You know I will."

He kissed her again and he believed her.

A minute later, his brother and Marco rolled up in a black Honda. DeVante climbed out of the car and said, "I see shawty growing a little ass. You hitting that?"

"Don't disrespect my girl."

"Bruh, that's a compliment, considering the small ass she had when you first started seeing her."

Brooke pulled him closer and kissed him again.

DeVante said, "You coming with us or you going to give us the work? We have money to make."

"I'm coming. Just give me a moment."

DeVante climbed in the car. DeMontre's hand still held a firm grip on Brooke's ass.

"Don't go," Brooke said.

"Nothing is going to happen."

"You don't know that."

"Don't think negative."

"Ok. I'm going to think positive."

"Negative Nancy!"

She smiled and kissed him again. "When am I going to see you again?"

"Tomorrow."

"You promise?"

"I promise."

"Perfect!"

He removed a thousand dollars from his pocket and passed it to her.

"What is this for?"

"Go buy yourself something nice."

She attempted to give him the money back. "You know I can't keep this. My mom will know if I buy something."

"I didn't say spend it all at one time. You have a job, Brooke."

"I know; I save most of my money."

"Well, save this."

She folded the bills and tucked them in her purse.

Marco blew the horn.

"I know you gotta go."

He kissed her forehead.

"Be safe, babe."

He climbed into the car with his brother and best friend.

She watched them as they darted out of the neighborhood. Damn she loved that boy.

Chapter 27

Nana called Black screaming and hollering.
"What's wrong?"
"Get over here! Come over here now!"
Black screamed into the phone, "Tell me what's going on!"
Nana was sobbing. "Oh Jesus. Help me, Lord. Help me, Lord."
"I'm on my way over there right now," he said, but Nana had already hung up the phone.
Black's sister, Rashida, telephoned him. "Hello?"
"You talk to Nana?"
"I'm on my way over there."
"Me too."
"Did she tell you what was wrong?"
"No. I called Asia and her phone keeps going to voice mail."
"Damn. She has a new man; she probably out with him."
"Tierany had a phone but her mom took it away."
Black's phone rang. His father.
"Pop is on the other line. I will see you at Nana's." Black clicked over.
"Hey, boy. What the hell is going on?"
"I don't know."

"I'm on my way to Nana's. She called me crying but wouldn't tell me what was going on. I thought she was supposed to be in Mississippi with her sister."

"I was going to send her tomorrow," Black said. "I'm trying to get in touch with Asia. Can I call you back?"

"I'll see you at Nana's."

Nana's house was surrounded by the cops and when Black spotted the yellow crime tape, he knew that something had gone horribly wrong. He parked above the neighbor's driveway and rushed out of the car, pushing through a throng of people who had gathered on the street to watch.

Chad Bailey, Black's middle school teammate, was the cop standing by the rope. "You can't come past the tape, Black."

"This is my Nana's house."

Black spotted Nana sitting on the porch in a chair talking to two plainclothes cops. "Nana."

She turned and when she saw him. Nana said, "That's my grandbaby. He lives here."

The plainclothes ordered the uniform to let Black past the tape.

Nana hugged Black and he asked what the hell was going on. She shook her head as tears rolled down her face.

"What happened, Nana?"

"The babies are gone."

"What do you mean? Somebody took my kids? Somebody kidnapped them?"

"No, baby, they are gone! Gussie brought me home from church, and when I came in the house, I saw three dead bodies." Gussie was Nana's best friend, and at eighty years old, she still drove.

"Three dead bodies?"

"The kids and Asia. All murdered."

Black's posture sank and he said, "Please tell me you're lying, Nana. Tell me you're lying."

She stroked his hair like she did when he was a baby and said, "They are with the Lord, son."

"Where are the bodies?"

She turned and faced the house and said, "They're inside, baby."

Black sprinted into the house and spotted a few Xbox video games on the floor, along with a Samsung tablet that belong to Tierany. One adult and two child-sized body bags.

Black made his way over to where the paramedic was stooped over. The man looked up and made eye contact with Black. His nametag said Peterson. He was a tall, lanky man with auburn-colored hair and deep blue concerned eyes.

Black said, "I need to see my kids."

"I'm so sorry. I'm sorry this happened to you." Peterson called his supervisor, a heavy-set Hispanic man named Sanchez.

Sanchez said it was okay for Black to take a look.

Black then kneeled to touch his daughter.

Peterson unlocked the bag and Black kneeled over and kissed Tierany. He could see the bullet wound on the side of her face and the dried, crimson-colored blood.

"My baby girl. I'm so, so sorry." He held her head for a moment and brushed her hair with his hands before kissing her on the jaw.

Peterson zipped Tierany's bag then unzipped Asia's.

She appeared to be sleeping peacefully. The beautiful hair, which Black had fallen in love with, covered her face. He removed her hair and kissed her on the forehead. He searched her body for the gunshot wound. He asked Peterson where the wound was located.

"Looks like it entered her back and came out the chest."

Black kissed her.

Peterson unzipped the final body bag and Black saw Man-Man's tiny little body. His shirt was soaked with blood and the side of his face disfigured.

"My baby boy!!" He held his son and his body propped over Black's knee. He planted a kiss on his son's face. He kissed him again, remembering how it was when Man-Man was a baby; he would wake up and his son would be smiling, and he'd be kissing Black all over his face.

"I love you, son."

Peterson and Sanchez felt bad for Black but they remaining stone-faced. They'd witnessed scenes like this so many times. It was part of their business.

Sanchez said, "I don't mean to be insensitive, but we have to go."

Black looked up at Sanchez. "Thank you for this. I appreciate it."

The man nodded and said, "We have to finish doing our work."

Black thanked the man and headed out the door. He pushed through the crowd that was positioned around the tape. Inside the rental car was the bracelet his daughter had asked him for. Seconds later, he was inside Nana's house again, and he asked Peterson for permission to give his daughter the bracelet.

The paramedic looked at him and felt bad for him, but he said, "Let me ask my supervisor." He waved Sanchez over once more.

"He wants to know if he could give the smaller girl a bracelet."

"I'm sorry, we can't allow that."

"All I want to do is give her this. No more kisses or nothing."

"I can't allow that."

"What is going to hurt?"

"I can't do it. I'm sorry."

There was a plainclothes cop walking by. Black grabbed him around the waist and snatched his gun. He quickly put the gun up to the cop's head.

Bailey, Black's childhood friend, drew his gun and said, "What the hell are you doing, man?" Bailey pointed the gun at Black.

"I want to give my daughter this bracelet," he said in a low voice.

"Let the officer go and drop the gun."

Black's father and sister arrived. After they saw what was going on, they both pleaded at the same time, "Please, Black, let him go."

"I can't. I need to give this to my daughter." Tears were moisturizing his cheeks.

"You can give it to her when she gets to the funeral," his sister said.

"Please, son. Don't do nothing stupid. Do you want to die

too?"

"I don't give a fuck if I die."

"This ain't the way to handle it."

Nana burst into house and said, "Tyrann, you drop that gun right now. You hear me, boy!"

She made her way up to him and he said, "Get away from me, Nana."

"What are you going to do to me, Tyrann? Kill me? No, drop that gun."

"Nana, get away."

"I won't."

Nana was face to face with Black, who had the gun beside the trembling officer's head. "Drop the gun and nobody has to get hurt."

Black glanced at Bailey. He'd always been fair. Black released the man, kneeled, and dropped the gun.

Seconds later, five officers rushed Black and hogtied him. In no time, they had loaded him into the back of the police car.

Chapter 28

TeTe received a call from an unknown number. Her first thought was not to answer it, but at the last moment, she decided to answer. "Hello."

"TeTe, you don't know me, but this is Black's sister, Rashida."

"Is there something wrong?"

"There is." She breathed heavily.

"What happened? Where is Black?"

"Black is in jail."

"What do you mean he's in jail? What is he in jail for?"

"Black's baby mama, Asia, and two of his children were murdered today."

"What! Please tell me you're kidding!"

"I wish I was, but it's the truth."

"How did he end up in jail?"

"He grabbed one of the officer's gun and tried to demand that they let him see his daughter."

"Damn," TeTe said. Her mind went back to the day that she'd met Black's children. The day that Black's baby mother had set him up. She didn't particularly care for that woman, but she was sad about her death. She was sad for Black.

"Did Black tell you to call me?"

"Yeah, he wants you to get in touch with his attorney. I don't know about that kind of stuff, and he told me to tell you that he'll be calling you at eight o'clock tonight."

"Thank you, honey."

"Thanks for being there for my brother."

• • •

DeMontre, DeVante, and Marco were on interstate I-26 when they noticed the Georgia State Patrol behind them. Marco checked the review mirror then switched lanes. The trooper switched lanes.

DeMontre was now panicking because not only did he have coke, he had guns and he was still attending classes. He took a lot of slow, deep breaths and tried to calm himself down.

"Slow down, he's going to go past you."

"Dude, I'm going the speed limit. He is not going to go past us. He's going to pull us."

DeVante said to DeMontre, "Give me the gun. I'm blasting this fool if we get pulled. What choice do we have?"

"We can't do all that moving and shifting; he might not even be thinking about pulling us over."

"We are going to get pulled."

The siren came on and they pulled to the side of the road.

Seconds later, a tall, long-faced Georgia State trooper named Carter approached the side of the car and barked, "License and registration."

Marco passed him the license and registration.

Carter studied the paper work then glanced in the backseat and made eye contact with DeMontre. He shined his flashlight on a fidgety DeMontre. "You look nervous back there, son."

Silence.

"Have you guys been smoking?"

"No, sir, we haven't."

"Tell me the truth."

"No, sir."

"There's no drugs in this car?"

"Why did you pull us over in the first place?" DeVante said.

DeMontre stared at his brother without saying anything, but his gaze said, Shut the fuck up.

Carter returned to his cruiser long enough to check the information and call for backup.

DeVante said to DeMontre, "We need to kill this motherfucker right now, homie. Give me the gun, I'll take him out."

"I can't let you throw your life away."

Now DeMontre thought about Brooke and how she had begged him not to leave. He wished he was at home cuddling with her right now.

DeVante said, "Give me the dope then, and I'll take off running."

DeMontre passed his brother a sandwich baggie filled with crack cocaine, and DeVante stuffed the drugs into his crotch.

Moments later, three more trooper cars approached the scene of the crime. Along with a K-9 unit.

Officer Carter ordered DeVante and DeMontre out of the car and walked them to the rear of the vehicle. The officer asked whether he could search the car.

"No."

"We're going to search it anyway."

"Why the fuck did you even ask?"

Carter's face was flush red. He nodded at another trooper, signaling for him to search the car.

DeVante looked at DeMontre and whispered, "Give me the gun."

"Are you fuckin crazy?"

"Man, I'm running."

The trooper was digging underneath the seat and spotted a capsule.

After examining the pill, he motioned another trooper to come examine it.

State Trooper Weiderman walked to the rear of the car and handed Carter the suspected drug. The pill was worth studying because the dog in the truck was trained to hunt, not detect drugs.

DeVante said to DeMontre, "I'm running."

"We can't leave Marco."

"He's good. I got the dope and you got the gun."

"You're right, but..."

"Let's go."

"We can't."

"I'm leaving. You with me or not?"

The officers were still studying the pill.

DeVante struck out running and DeMontre was right behind him.

Carter called it in as one other trooper drew his weapon and said, "Stop!"

The troopers got the dog and gave chase after the twins. The boys ran down a hill until they reached a branch of water filled with rocks. They would have to leap onto and across several rocks to cross the stream. DeMontre had leapt onto a rock in the middle of the water.

Footsteps and the sound of hounds were getting closer.

DeVante twisted his ankle and fell. He told his brother, "Keep running, bruh. Don't worry about me." He began digging in his shorts frantically trying to locate the drugs so he could lose them in the water. His ankle throbbed. His hands crawling down his pants, he finally felt the bag.

The dog was getting closer.

DeMontre was now on the other side of the creek, his brother lying in agony. He couldn't leave. What kind of brother would he be?

DeVante tore into the bag and dumped the drugs into his mouth and swallowed them. When he saw his brother coming he said, "Get out of here, bruh. I'm going to be okay."

DeMontre was not having it. Seconds later, he stood over his brother, grabbed his arm, and tried to pick him up.

The three officers arrived and stood a few feet away from them with their guns drawn. "Get down!"

DeMontre and DeVante lay face down staring at each other.

DeVante's heart was pounding fast and he said, "My chest hurt so bad, bruh." The drugs had already entered his blood stream.

DeMontre saw the whites of his brother's eyes.

"What's wrong, bruh?"

"I swallowed it."

"You swallowed what?"

"The dope."

DeMontre said, "Get my brother to the hospital!"

The cop said, "What's wrong?" as he turned him over on his side. DeVante's eyes were barely open, his tongue coated with coke residue. "Oh my God. He's swallowed some dope."

"My chest is on fire."

"Help my brother. Help him!" DeMontre shouted.

The officer grabbed him around his stomach and tried the Heimlich maneuver to get him to cough up the rocks.

DeVante made eye contact with his brother and said, "I love you, bruh." His body went limp.

DeMontre said, "Bruh? Don't die, bruh, don't die." He struggled to crawl toward his twin brother. His hands being cuffed from behind made the feat almost impossible. His face brushed against the dirt.

The officer touched DeVante's neck, taking his pulse. He looked at DeMontre and said, "I'm sorry, he's gone."

"Da fuck you mean, he's gone? Bring him back! Ain't you trained in CPR and shit like that?"

"There is nothing I can do."

"Try CPR."

The man kneeled and administered CPR for the next five minutes before finally giving up and saying it was useless.

Chapter 29

Meeka screamed into the phone, "My son is dead! My son is dead!"

"Wait. What?" Starr tried to process what her sister had just said to her. Did she say her son was dead? Who killed him? What happened? Was she dreaming? Is my nephew really dead?

"What did you just say?"

"DeVante is dead."

"Who killed him? What happened?"

All she could hear was her sister sobbing. This had to be a bad dream.

"Meeka, what happened to DeVante?"

She was crying. And Starr knew that she would have to call her parents to find out what was going on. She would have to call her father because Meeka couldn't speak; her son was dead. She thought about DeMontre. That dope that he had stolen from Q. She was sure this had something to do with it.

"Meeka, what happened?"

"The police," she cried. She kept crying. Stuttering as she was trying to explain what happened.

"The police killed DeVante?"

Starr hoped like hell that the police hadn't killed DeVante. Her father, Ace, had already vowed that if the police killed any of his offspring, there would be the Black Lives Matter rally for him. He had made a promise that if the police killed one of his, he was going to take out a few of them, and Starr believed him.

"Yeah...I mean, no."

"Calm down, sis."

She knew she sounded crazy for even trying to tell her sister to calm down. How could she keep calm when she had lost a child? Her own flesh and blood.

"Meeka, calm down." She heard Meeka breathing. She was trying to catch her breath.

"My son is gone."

"I know."

"Tell me what happened."

"The police got behind Marco, DeMontre, and DeVante. They jumped out and ran and DeMontre swallowed some rocks. I meant to say DeVante swallowed rocks and his heart stopped."

"Where's DeMontre?"

"In jail."

"For what?"

"Got caught wit' a gun."

"I'm coming over. Right now."

Meeka ended the call.

Starr drove to Jada's home. Jada was surprised to see her. She ushered her right in and said, "Is there something I can get you? You look a mess." Jada made eye contact with her friend, whose hair was disheveled. Her eyes were red and teary looking. "What's going on?"

"So much."

Jada led Starr to the kitchen and the two ladies sat at the bar. "My nephew died."

"Please tell me you're kidding."

Jada embraced Starr and held her tightly. "You poor baby, you."

Jada took her seat again.

I'm upset that my grandson is dead, but your sister didn't have anything to do with it."

Jada felt uncomfortable that they were airing out family issues. She excused herself.

"Jada, you don't have to go nowhere."

Meeka said, "Whatever I gotta say, I'll say it in front of Jada."

"What you gotta say?"

"Why don't you tell Mama and Daddy the real reason my son is dead today."

Starr stood there looking baffled, and both of her parents stared at her.

"What the hell are you talking about?"

"I'm talkin' about dat dope boy of yours giving my son work."

"What?" Starr said. She couldn't believe that this bitch had just sat there and lied.

"Q gave Montre drugs to sell."

"That ain't true," Jada said.

Meeka stared at Jada like she wanted to slap the shit out her, but she remembered how Jada had beat the shit out that girl at Trey's funeral and decided that that wouldn't be a good idea.

Starr said, "Q didn't give DeMontre shit. DeMontre stole the work, and Meeka know it."

"It don't matter; if you hadn't exposed my son to that dope boy, my baby would still be here." Then Meeka charged Starr and Jada got between them.

Meeka gave Jada the cold eye and said, "Get out the damn way, Jada. This is between two sisters."

"I understand that."

"If you understand that, then get the fuck out the way."

"I can't."

"Move." And Meeka tried to swing around her but Jada caught Meeka's hands.

"You need to get the hell out of the way."

"She's pregnant," Jada said.

"What?" This surprised Ace.

"Yeah, I was going to tell you," Starr said.

Wanda said, "I knew you was pregnant."

Meeka headed toward her bedroom and before she closed the door she said, "I hope your baby die like mine died."

Starr broke down into tears as Jada embraced her.

• • •

Joey Turch paced in the client-attorney room of the county jail. Black sat at the table, a defeated man, and he needed Turch more than ever to work one last miracle. He needed a bail set, but he had taken a policeman's weapon and held him hostage, though technically for only three minutes. They still charged him with holding an officer hostage.

He stared at Turch and said, "I'm going to need you to get me out of here."

Turch's eyebrows raised and he said, "Tyrann, we still got that matter of the fake coke that you sold, and now this new charge of holding an officer hostage. Nobody is going to give you a bond. I'm one of the best attorneys around, but I can't turn water into wine."

"Don't give me that best attorney in Atlanta shit because you're not the best. If you were the best, I'd be out now. You're not the best."

"Everybody is entitled to their opinion."

Black kneeled and cuffed the legs of his oversized county jail jumpsuit. Then he made eye contact with Turch. "Do you know what happened to me?"

"Yes. I know what happened but, Tyrann, there is no way I can get you out of here."

"I wanna go to my kids' funeral. I can't take it if they are buried without me saying my final goodbye. I am mentally checked out right now."

"I'm sorry."

Black was teary-eyed. "Get me a goddamn bond! I don't care if it's a million dollars. I need to get out of this motherfucker." His face was serious. "What part of that don't you understand?"

"I'll try."

"Do more than try, motherfucker. You work for me."

Black and Joey Turch made eye contact for a few seconds and then Black asked, "Do you know Agent Barry Daniels?"

"An FBI field agent. Transferred here from Texas. What about him?"

"Get in touch with him. He'll get me out."

"What are you talking about? Are you thinking of cooperating?"

"Just call him for me. Get in touch with him."

Turch said, "Are you sure you want to do this?"

"I need to give my kids their final goodbyes."

Chapter 31

It was 2:35 a.m. when the front desk called Starr and told her that she had a guest. It was Q again. She wanted them to turn him away, but she couldn't say it.

When she opened the door, they stared at each other awkwardly for a few moments. She said, "And you are here because?"

"I heard about what happened and I'm sorry." He paused and said, "I really didn't know DeVante that well. You know I knew DeMontre."

"You could have sent flowers. You didn't have to come, you know."

He thumbed his belt loops and rocked side to side, avoiding eye contact. What was he to say? Except he was sorry. He licked his lips and said, "How is Meek?"

"How do you think she's taking it? She has a dead son."

"Stupid-ass question, huh?"

"You're just trying to make conversation."

"I am."

"I'm glad you came."

His eyes widened. "Really?"

"I feel alone."

"You're not; I'm here." He took hold of her, and when she resisted, he let her go.

She said. "I don't know why I feel like this. I should hate you."

"I didn't kill Trey."

"I don't want to talk about that right now. I don't even want to think about that right now."

"I won't bring it up."

"Good."

She took a deep breath and said, "Meeka blamed me for DeVante's death. Can you believe that?"

"What?"

"She said you gave them the drugs and they were selling for you."

Q was nervous and ran his fingers through his hair and he said, "Who did she tell that to?"

"My parents."

"And who else?"

"Nobody."

"Are you sure?"

She laughed and said, "Nobody is snitching on you, Q."

"Why did she blame you?"

"She's upset! You know people say shit they don't mean when they are upset."

"I know you don't want to be with me. I understand that, but can you let me be there for you until you get through this?"

She smiled. "I'd like that."

●   ●   ●

The smell of rain was inside the visitation room. TeTe played solitaire on her cellphone as she waited for Black to come out. She didn't believe in social media, thought of it as a waste of time and a distraction. Besides, motherfuckers didn't need to know what she was doing every moment of the day.

After three games of solitaire, the jailer brought Black out. A glass partition separated them. He smiled when he saw her. He picked up the telephonic receiver. She picked up seconds later.

"Hey, baby."

"You heard what happened?"

"Yeah."

"Careful what you say." TeTe knew that the conversation was being monitored. She glanced at a fat-ass jailer munching on flaming hot Cheetos. "So what's going on?"

"No bond. Can you believe this shit?"

She sighed and said, "I gotta get you out of here somehow."

"Tell me about it."

"You have to go to the funeral."

He dropped his head and said, "I have to come to grips with the fact that they may not let me out."

"Damn, baby."

Black ran his fingers through his locks. "I know. I just lost it. Just imagine that you lost your kid."

"I don't want to think about that."

"Have you ever seen two small body bags?"

"No."

"I had to witness that shit. I had to see a hole in my son's head."

"Look on the bright side: if you don't make bond at least you don't have to see two small caskets."

"That's one way to look at it." Black met her eyes and he looked intense. "I gotta get out of here or I'm going to go crazy. I swear to God, babe, I can't take it."

"What can I do to get you out of here?"

"I need an attorney."

"I thought you had the best attorney in Atlanta."

He wanted to tell her to get in touch with FBI Agent Daniels, but he knew better than to ask her to do that. She would absolutely not do that.

"I thought so too. But the motherfucker can't get me out."

"I will do anything for you, babe."

"I know you will. But just know that if I don't get to see my children one more time, I'll never be right again."

"You're lucky you have more kids; I only have one."

"But those were my babies. The ones that I spent the most time with."

"And their mama is dead?"

"Yeah."

"You know how I felt about that bitch." TeTe scowled.

"I need you to do two things. Contact your attorney and see if he can get me out of this hell hole."

"And what's the other thing?"

"Find Champagne."

"For what?"

"See if she knows somebody that knows our friends. When you find them, take care of that."

TeTe knew that Black didn't want to say too much, but she knew that Black wanted those Detroit boys dead. She didn't have to find Champagne; she knew exactly where she was. She had been fucking and sucking Asian businessmen for the last three days.

Black pressed his hand against the glass and she put her hand against the partition and whispered, "I love you."

Chapter 32

Champagne sat on a chair bound by a rope when TeTe entered the room with two henchmen and two pit bulls. One grey and the other one brown. Caleb could barely hold the dogs. Champagne was sweating and she squirmed in the chair.

TeTe stood directly in front of her and said, "Untie her."

One of the henchman untied her.

Champagne said, "I don't understand. Why are you doing me like this? I've done everything that you asked me to do."

"Except..."

"What haven't I done?"

"You didn't tell me where the Detroit boys are."

The loud sound of the dogs barking was beginning to annoy TeTe. She turned to Caleb and said, "Make them shut the fuck up."

When the dogs stopped barking, TeTe said, "Tell me where the Detroit boys at or I swear to God, bitch, I'll let these dogs rip the white meat off yo ass." She kneeled until she was face to face with her. "Do you think I'm playing?"

"No."

"I've been good to you, haven't I?"

Champagne knew that TeTe hadn't been good to her, but she did let her live. Of course, she'd had her selling pussy all day every day. "I don't know where those dudes are. I told you that already."

"Did you hear what happened to Black?"

"No. Please tell me that Black is still living."

"He is."

Champagne let out sigh of relief. "Me and Black are friends."

The dogs barked again and Champagne twitched. And she kept flinching.

"Two of Black's kids were murdered along with his babies' mother."

"Oh no." Champagne became teary eyed and said, "I'm so sorry. Is that why Black is in jail? Did he retaliate?"

"How in the hell can he retaliate if he don't know where to retaliate? And besides, didn't you hear me say that he was in jail?"

"I did."

TeTe turned to Caleb and said, "Bring them closer."

He made his way over and stood directly in front of Champagne; she could see the jagged teeth of the pit bulls.

"A-T-T-A-C-K will make them rip the flesh off your bones. Do you understand me?"

"I do."

"Do you understand me, bitch?"

"I do."

I don't think you do."

She nodded. "What do you want me to do?"

"I want you to take your ass to the club tonight. As a matter of fact, I want you to go all week. Caleb is going to be your escort, and I want you to find a bitch that knows where the hell these niggas are. Or else your ass is done."

She nodded. Caleb held up a doll in front of the dog and said, "Attack," and the dogs ripped the doll's head off and shredded it into tiny pieces.

TeTe grinned and said, "If you don't get me what I want, that's going to be your ass the next time."

Chapter 33

After DeVante's funeral, church members and family gathered at Starr's parents' house. Jada, Brooke, and even Fresh had come through to show their support. Shamari called Starr from prison and Black was in the county jail still dealing with his own problems.

The doorbell rang. Ace sprang from his seat and opened the door. He saw that it was Q and said, "Get the fuck away from my house."

"I came to offer my condolences."

"You can't be serious, motherfucker. It's your dope that killed my grandbaby."

Q shrugged and said, "I understand how you must feel."

Ace said, "Nigga, you have no idea how I must feel. But if you be here when I come back, your mama is going to understand how I must feel. Ace disappeared into the back and retrieved a .45 Magnum. When he returned, Q was standing there with a Glock 29.

"You want to talk like men?" Q said.

Ace drew his gun then the two stood there staring at each other. "You want to kill each other?"

Meeka entered the room and screamed, "Daddy, what are

y'all doing?"

Starr's mother, Wanda, came running to the living room. "Ace, put that damn gun down!"

Ace said, "You tell him to put his goddamned gun down. I ain't putting down shit."

Q lowered his gun and said to them all, "I just came to offer my condolences."

Wanda took the gun from Ace.

DeMontre said, "Granddaddy, you can't blame Uncle Q. If there is anybody to blame, it's me. I took his shit. I stole his dope. I shouldn't have done it. It's karma. I just wish I was the one that died instead of my brother. It's my fault that he's gone."

Brooke stroked his shoulders.

Meeka turned to Starr and said, "I'm sorry for what I said to you earlier, sis." Then she said to Q, "Come in the house and get you a plate, since you're going to be a part of the family."

"I am?"

"My sister has your baby, right?"

"Yes, she does." Q and Starr smiled. There was no way that she wanted to reveal to her parents that their baby was actually someone else's. Someone that they had not met.

Jada grinned.

Ace made his way over to Q and extended his hand. "I'm sorry."

"Not an issue. You were just doing what you had to do to protect your family."

"I'm going to always do that."

"As you should. Like I said, I'm so sorry for what happened. If there is anything I can do to help, I will."

• • •

Black was lying on the top bunk. Still no bond and today was the day that they were laying his kids and baby mother to rest. He hopped off the bed. He needed to talk to someone in the outside world or he was going to drive himself insane. There was a dude on the county jail phone and Black recognized him right away. It was Bird, the man who had taken his money and had Avant murdered right in front of him.

Bird was sitting in a chair with his back toward Black. Black grabbed an empty chair in front of a phone booth behind Bird. He bashed Bird's head with the chair and Bird stumbled to the floor. Bird tried to regain his balance but couldn't because he was wearing shower shoes. Black kicked him in the mouth, knocking Bird's head against a cement block. Bird rose to his feet and grinned when he saw Black, then he squared up.

The pudgy officer had been reading a Men's Fitness magazine when he heard the fuss. He bolted toward the fight but inmates formed a wall that prevented the officer from getting any closer.

Black said, "Fight me, motherfucker."

A tall guy with long plaits stood beside Bird and said, "Let's get this motherfucker, homie."

A huge dude with a scar on the left side of his face named Monster said, "Let the two of them fight. Anybody else jump in, I'm shanking dey ass." He flashed gold teeth and an evil grin.

Black and Bird squared off in the center. Bird charged Black with his head down. Black grabbed him by the head and power drove him into the concrete floor, face-first. Then Black flipped him on his back and kicked him in the ribs. When Bird rose to his feet, Monster stuck him six times.

More than a dozen prison guards raided the jail and ordered everybody to get down. They fired rubber bullet guns. A jailer with a bullhorn ordered everyone to lie on the floor. Everyone was ordered to return to their assigned bunk areas, and Bird was hauled off to the hospital. On a stretcher.

Chapter 34

The pod had been locked down for three days following the fight, and Black had been resting on the top bunk reading the Godsend Series by K. Elliott when a guard said, "Tyrann Massey, get your things. You bailed out today."

"What? This can't be true. I don't even have a bond. How did I make bond?"

"Just get your things."

Black jumped off the bed and began giving all his belongings to his cellmates. A bunch of soups and stamps. Black gave away all his belongings.

It took him thirty minutes to get processed out. He stepped out the door and powered on his cellphone.

Daniels called. "You wanna thank me now or later?"

"What?"

"How do you think you got out?"

"Joey Turch contacted you?"

"He did."

"Why didn't you get me out for my kids' funeral?"

"You have one of the worst criminal records in Atlanta."

"How did you pull it off?"

"Told them you were on special assignment."

"So they think I'm a snitch?"

"Hey, you're out."

"This is true."

"So what are you doing?"

"I just got out, you know that."

"Where are you?"

"Up the street from the jail."

"I'll come get you and drop you off somewhere."

"I don't need to be seen with you."

"The window is tinted."

"Okay. I'm at the corner of Rice and Niles."

"I'll be in a white Jeep Wagoneer."

"Ah'ight."

Black called TeTe. No answer.

Seconds later, Daniels rolled up in a white SUV. Black climbed into the car.

"They weren't going to let you out unless I said that you were going to work for me."

"I understand and I needed to be out."

"To get revenge?"

"Smart man. Nobody does shit like that to me and get away."

"I got you out so we can make some money."

"Of course you did."

"I'm about to get some big-time Mexicans. They're heavy in the game."

"I see." Black heard Daniels but his mind was on the Detroit boys. There was no way he was going to let them get away with what they had done.

"Drop me off on the West Side. I need to see my family."

"I got you."

They rode in silence before Daniels said, "The doctor recanted his statement about your friend."

"Oh yeah?"

"So there is no need to give him shit. I took care of that for you."

"How did you get him to do that?"

"He's locked up in PC and there is a biker gang after his ass. I just threatened to put his ass in General Population."

"So when is my boy getting out?"

"That's up for the court to decide. If he gets out at all. You know he had other charges."

When he reached Glenwood, Black hopped out of the car.

Chapter 35

Jada texted Fresh: I need to be touched.

Fresh: *I'm coming right over.*

When Fresh entered Jada's town home, she was wearing nothing but a matching thong and bra set. He stood there in awe of her incredible body, and nervous at the same time. The last time they had seen each other had been at Starr's mother's house and Jada had barely spoken to him.

"I thought you had a man?"

"My man has a woman."

"You're a side chick?"

"He's a side nigga."

"You're crazy as hell, girl."

She inched toward him. "Did you miss me?"

"You know I did." He pulled her closer. His hands on the small of her back.

"You didn't speak to me at Starr's mother's house."

"You barely looked my way. I did speak, though."

"I was trying not to look at your sexy ass."

She kissed him and his hands were gripping her ass. She pulled him by the shirt and led him into the bedroom.

He sat on the edge of the bed. "What's up with that dude

anyway? He was the dude I saw you with at the game that time. He's been around for a while; you like him?"

"Why?"

"It's just a question."

She disappeared without answering him and returned wearing absolutely nothing. His mouth flew open.

"What did you want to know?"

He tried not to look her way. "Do you like that dude?"

"Maybe."

"What's his name? I forgot."

"Does it matter?"

"You told me once; I just forgot."

"His name is Tank."

"So you like Tank?"

"Tank has someone."

"But if he didn't have a woman?"

"If he didn't have a woman I could see myself being with a man like Tank."

"That's all I'm asking."

"Does that bother you?"

"Maybe."

"Wait a minute. You're the one that said that you didn't want anything serious."

"I know I did."

Jada crawled in the bed like a kitten and said, "Let's not talk about that right now." Her nipples were rock hard.

He kicked off his shoes and crawled into the bed with her. She unfastened his belt and began giving him head.

With his head tilted back, he said, "I can't believe I'm here."

She stopped. "Do you not want to be here?"

"I do."

"What's the matter?"

"I don't know, Jada. Ever since I seen you with that dude, it has made me want you more."

"You want what you can't have?"

He smiled. "I can't have you?"

"You can have my body, but you can't have my heart and mind."

"Yeah. I never thought I would be in this space."

"It's called an emotional attachment."

"Oh yeah?"

"Yeah. Now quit talking." She pushed him back and continued to suck him until he climaxed. He then dozed off without sexing her. She was pissed that she didn't get hers. At least she had a warm body in her bed.

She woke up early and hopped in the shower. When Fresh heard the sound of the shower running, he rolled over and spotted her cell phone on the counter and checked her text. The last time she'd heard from Tank was two days ago...

Jada: *I miss you.*

Tank: *I miss you too.*

Jada: *Did you get a chance to put that money in my account?*

Tank: *You miss me or my money?*

Jada: *I miss you of course but I need money.*

Jada: *When am I going to see you?*

Tank: *I don't know, doing shit with the fam all day.*

Jada: *You're full of shit.*

Tank: *I'll make it up to you.*

Jada: *Have a good day, daddy.*

He was about to put the phone down before he thought, Let me see who else she has been texting. The only other person that she had been texting was Starr, and the last text was at 5:45 a.m.

Starr: *I think I'm going to abort the baby today.*

Jada: *Oh no!!!*

Starr: *I think it's best!!*

Jada: *But your parents are so happy. They want you to have the baby.*

Starr: *They think it's Q's of course.*

Jada: *I know, but I couldn't help but think how happy they were when they found out that you were having a baby.*

Starr: *You mean when you blurted it out.*

Jada: *My bad.*

Starr: *I ain't tripping.*

Jada: *But you know they just lost a grandson so I was kind of happy for them!*

Starr: *This is my life and I can't let them dictate what's good for me or my son.*

Jada: *I feel you.*

Starr: *If you can come with me, I would appreciate it.*

Jada: *What kind of question is that? Of course I'll come with you. What time?*

Star: *10:30. Be at my house at 9:45 I want you to drive me.*

Jada: *Okay.*

When Jada stepped into the bedroom. She found Fresh fully dressed and she said, "You're not washing your ass?"

"You crazy, girl." He laughed and said, "I have to go."

"You think I am." Jada knew that the trap niggas didn't always wash their asses, always on the go. But she'd never seen Fresh not take a shower. She said, "Let me hook you up with some breakfast real fast."

He leaned into her and kissed her on the jaw and said, "I gotta go."

"You know you owe me."

"Huh?"

"Bruh! You dozed last night without me even getting mine. What kind of shit is that?"

"I know."

"Bye, boy."

Chapter 36

The abortion clinic was located on Piedmont Avenue. Starr and Jada arrived to a crowd of pro-lifers standing and waving signs concerning dead fetuses.

A tear trickled down Starr's face and Jada said, "Don't pay them motherfuckers no mind. You gotta do what you gotta do!"

A white man approached the car holding a sign that read: Conception starts at ejaculation. His red face was now pressed against the window and he said, "Killers!"

Jada removed a small handgun from her purse and pointed at the man. "Back the fuck away from the car."

Seconds later, another white woman approached and Jada said, "Bitch, what do you want?"

"My name is Mary Austin. I'm with the clinic. I need you to follow me, and we can park behind the clinic so you can get away from these lunatics."

Starr followed the woman to the back of the clinic. When they stepped out of the car and were heading into the clinic, Starr heard someone call her name. She turned and saw that it was Q. What the fuck was he doing here?

"I want to talk."

The clinic rep looked nervous.

"It's okay, Mary," Starr said.

"You need me?" Jada asked.

"No. Let me talk to him alone."

Mary said to Jada, "You can come in here and have a seat in the lobby."

Jada said, "Wait a minute. I ain't the one pregnant."

"I know." The woman smiled politely.

Jada trailed Mary inside the building.

Starr stared at Q and there were so many emotions going through her head. She loved this man. She hated him. He was her hero and she was glad he had been there for her when her nephew had died. She was happy he had been there for her family and they all were happy that they thought he was the father of her child.

"Why are you here?"

"Hopefully to talk you out of something crazy."

"How did you know I was here? Did Jada run her mouth?"

"I followed you."

"What? Why?"

"I didn't intentionally follow you. But I was coming over and then I saw you and Jada pull out of your building parking lot and I trailed y'all."

"That's crazy."

"No, what's crazy is that you're here and you don't need to be here."

"What do you mean I don't need to be here?"

"You need to have this baby."

"Why should I have the baby? And why do you care? You have children, Q, out in Texas that you don't raise. Why would you care about what I do?"

"I care about you."

"You want me to have another man's baby? I know you've been saying that, but I never believed you."

"What do I have to do to prove it to you? I'm here and I don't want you to abort this child."

"This child has a father. A father that will be a part of his life if I have it. He'll have that right."

"I know."

"You can deal with that?"

"Don't abort a baby because of what I can or can't deal with."

"Of course not, silly. I want a baby, but I just don't want to be alone with this."

"But you said your baby's father was going to be in the baby's life."

"You know what I mean."

"I'm here for you."

"But you are a drug lord. Who knows how long you will be around?"

"Who knows how long anyone will be around? Life is about chances."

Starr looked confused. She was standing there trying to understand him.

"I want you to have the baby. I'm going to be there for you."

"What about him?"

"Who?"

"The basketball player."

"You can co-parent with him."

The fact that he was so understanding made him the most amazing man that she had ever met. There was no way that most men would ever want the woman they loved to have another man's child.

Q stood with his hands in his pockets. Their eyes met and held and he said, "Just think about it. Give it one week and if you still feel this way after a week, I'll be the first to say come back and do it."

Jada peeked outside and said, "So what's it going to be?"

"She's not going to go through with it," Q said.

Jada said, "Good, after what your parents have gone through, I think it's a good idea that you keep the baby."

Mary stepped outside and said to Starr, "When you come back inside, I'm going to need you to fill out the paperwork and wait to speak to the counselor."

Starr said, "I changed my mind."

Chapter 37

Toby was a tall, husky man with a slightly gray beard. He was at the door of Club Onyx. He frisked Black and found a gun. Black slid him a hundred-dollar bill and Toby let him in with the weapon.

Black stood in the corner alone. He had been staying with his father but he had to get out of the house or else he would go crazy thinking about his children. A blonde with huge titties and ass made her way up to him and said, "You want a dance?"

"No."

"Want some company?"

"No."

"Why the stank attitude?"

Black examined the woman's body. Blondie had just the kind of body he loved. Skinny waist and a fantastic ass. Her titties were huge and natural with fat pink nipples. But he wasn't thinking about women. Otherwise, he would have made a proposition to Blondie and would have paid her to leave the club. And would have fucked her.

He gave her an empty stare. "My kids were just murdered."

"Oh my God. I think I saw something like that on the news.

Did it happen a few weeks ago?"

"Yeah."

"Why are you even here?"

"I don't know, thinking I could get my mind off this shit somehow."

"I want to dance for you for free."

Though Black wasn't in the mood for a dance, he thought Blondie was a nice girl. He handed her a hundred-dollar bill."

"What's this for?"

"You seem like a cool chick."

She smiled, revealing bottom level gold grill.

Thank you. She extended her hand and said, "What is your name?"

"Black."

"There is a thousand Black's in Atlanta. With a name like Black, you have to be in the game."

"What game?"

"You know what I'm talking about?"

"My kids just got murdered, you think that's a game?"

"No."

"And why are you asking me about the game anyway? Are you the Feds?"

Blondie looked at him oddly and said, "It was just conversation, brother. Chill the fuck out."

Black laughed and said, "I took it to another level, didn't I?"

"Yes, you did."

Do you know a girl named Champagne?"

"Yes."

"Where is she working tonight?"

"She's in the back getting dressed."

"Would you go get her for me?"

"So you wanna get a dance from that bird and not me?"

Black passed her another hundred and said, "Can you go get her for me?"

Seconds later Champagne came running to Black's table and hugged him and said, "I'm so sorry this happened to you."

"It's not your fault."

"When did you get out?"

"How did you know I was in jail?"

"Your crazy girlfriend tried to kill me." She didn't immediately answer the question.

"What?"

"She kidnapped me and had me turning tricks for her. Then when your kids got murdered…"

Black closed his eyes. Hearing the words broke him down.

"I'm sorry."

"Just hard for me getting used to hearing that."

"I bet."

"So what were you saying?"

"She picked me up and said she was going to kill me because I knew that you killed Sapphire. (TeTe was gonna kill Champagne because she thought she knew where the Detroit Boys were pg 147) But, Black, you know me. You know I don't get down like that. You know I ain't going to say shit about you to the po-po. I love you. I got love for you."

"I know."

"She had me selling ass. But you know that bitch is crazy. A few days ago, she showed up to my place. She was the one that told me about what happened to your kids. She took me to a place and threatened to let two pit bulls eat me alive."

"I don't believe you."

"Black, I don't lie. She wanted me to find out where those Detroit boys were but the only bitch that knew them was Sapphire. But there was a bitch named Roxy that use to dance at Pink Pony that used to fuck one of them Detroit boys."

"How do you know?"

"Sapphire mentioned that they had taken them down to South Beach and tricked on them."

"Where is Roxy?"

"I don't know. After TeTe threatened me with the pit bulls, I went to Pink Pony and asked about her and they said she ain't work there no more, so I don't know where she is."

"Roxy? That's all you know about her?"

"I think she's from Memphis."

"Okay."
"Tell that crazy bitch to leave me alone."
"Don't worry about her."
"I have to worry."

Chapter 38

Q and Fresh sipped Courvoisier on his terrace overlooking the city of Atlanta. Q told Fresh that he had agreed to take care of Starr's baby.

"You're a good man, brother."

"I love Starr."

Fresh turned to Q and sipped his drink. "I know you do. But I don't know if I could agree to take care of another man's child."

"We ask women to do it all the time."

Fresh took a swig. "You're right."

"I know I'm right."

Fresh shielded his face from the sun. "I have a question for you, big brother."

"What?" Q made his way over to the bar and poured a shot of liquor and downed it. "What you wanna know?"

"Why did you want Trey dead? Tell me the truth."

The two men looked at each other for a very long time before Q said, "Promise that you won't tell anyone."

"I promise."

"There was a dude named Monte that had got busted with a lot of work. He was Trey's runner."

"He went to prison."

"Yes. But dumb-ass Monte had gotten busted in a rental car and he'd rented the car from the same place for three years. All of this was revealed in the investigation and Monte had called Trey 130 times leading up to the day of the bust. The Feds ain't stupid. They knew that Monte and Trey were working together. Trey was on the Feds' radar."

"How do you know for sure?"

"Monte told me. Told me that they kept pressing him about Trey."

"And you thought Trey would give you up?"

"No. I never thought that for one minute, but it was cartel orders."

"Diego?"

"No, Ramon." Ramon was Diego and Gordo's uncle. "So it was either I kill Trey or they kill my entire family. So when the crazy white bitch killed him, I was happy. I wasn't happy that he was dead but I was happy that I didn't have to do it."

"But you lied to Starr."

"She wouldn't have understood. Trey was the reason I wanted out of the game. I'd been ordered to kill before, but never someone that I cared about."

Fresh said, "Speaking of Diego, he don't want to give me any work."

"Why not?"

"Says he doesn't have any."

"I told you to leave him alone and work with me."

"I don't get it."

Q laughed at Fresh and said, "Just do what I say; it's going to all work out in the end."

Fresh gave Q a pound.

•   •   •

The smell of lavender was in the air. Black examined Jada but not in a sexual way. He was just happy to see a familiar face. Someone that he considered to be a good friend.

Jada embraced him. "I'm so sorry about what happened. Are you okay?"

"Yeah, I'm fine. Just still trying to wrap my mind around the fact that they are gone."

"I don't know what you're feeling, but I can imagine that it's pretty bad."

Black didn't feel like talking about the situation, but he didn't want to be rude to Jada. He knew that she had his best interest at heart.

"Anything that you need from me, just let me know."

He bit his lip and said, "That means a lot."

"I sent some flowers to your Nana, but I wasn't able to attend the funerals. Too many people are dying; Starr's nephew even died."

"What? One of the twins?"

"Yeah."

"What do you mean he died? The one that took the coke from Q?"

"The other one."

"Tell Starr I send my condolences," Black said.

"She knows that you're going through some shit."

"You know, Starr is a good person. She don't deserve this."

"You don't deserve this either."

"My kids didn't deserve to die, but I deserve everything that I'm getting."

"Don't say that."

"It's the truth. So many people have lost their life because of me."

Black and Jada stared at each other. Jada wanted to say something to nullify what Black had said, but he'd spoken the truth. Everything that had happened to those babies had been because of him.

"Black, you have to let that go. You're still here. You know what I mean?"

"You're right."

"So what else is up? Would you like a drink?"

"No. I'm not going to be here long. I just needed to see a familiar face. We've been knowing each other for a long time and you were always cool to me."

She smiled then hugged Black again. She released him.

He said, "Did you take the attorney the money?"

"Yes."

"Damn."

"Why do you say damn?" she asked.

"Because your boy who confessed had already taken back his statement."

"But, Black, I had no choice. When I found out that you were in jail, the day was approaching and I had to do what I had to do."

"And now I have to do what I have to do."

The doorbell rang. Black looked at Jada and asked, "Were you expecting company?"

"Fresh." She eased a way over to the door and Black stole a look at her ass. What was she wearing?

Fresh hugged Black when he entered the house. "You okay, bruh?"

"I'm going to be okay."

"I wanted to talk about something with you."

Jada said, "I have to finish putting my makeup on."

After Jada excused herself, Fresh said, "You remember the dude that you stopped and asked to deal with you?"

"The plug?"

"Yeah."

"What about him?"

"I want to kill him."

"Why?"

"Long story. Can you help me?"

"I need to know why and what's in it for me."

"This dude has over a thousand bricks of coke. I'll split it with you."

"Why are you going to kill this motherfucker?"

"You with it or not?"

I'm not killing nobody. I got enough shit to think about." He looked at him with sincere eyes. "You know what I'm going through."

"I know what happened to you and I'm sorry; but guys like you and me, we just don't walk away from the game. You know how it goes."

"I never said I was walking away from anything. But when those niggas took the life of my innocent babies, I knew that karma had caught up with me. Everything that I have ever loved is gone, except for my Nana."

"So you can't help?"

"I can get someone to help you, but I need to know why. Why do you want this motherfucker dead?"

"He murdered a good friend."

"A good friend?" Black laughed. He didn't believe Fresh. It sounded like a lie, considering he'd just seen him out having dinner with the plug about a month earlier.

"Decapitated him."

"No shit?"

"And FedEx'd the head to Q."

"When?"

"Months ago."

Black studied Fresh's face to see if he saw signs of lying. He surely didn't look like he was lying. Black said, "Let me think about it."

Fresh embraced Black again and said, "Just let me know. Either way I'm cool with it."

Chapter 39

"I love you, baby. I love you so much!" TeTe said to Black as she held him.

When she released Black, he said, "I'm so glad to see you."

"So how did you get out?"

"The charges were dismissed; the judge had sympathy for me," Black lied. He didn't feel like revealing the details about how Daniels got him out. "Where is Butterfly?"

"With her Auntie." She massaged his chest and said, "Did you miss me?"

"Of course."

"You're acting kind of stand-offish."

"I just lost my babies. I'm sorry I'm not in the mood to fuck right now. I got other shit to do. I got money to make. I need to find the motherfuckers that did this. Do you understand?"

She tried to unbuckle his pants but he brushed her off and she made a sad face.

"Are you listening to me?"

"Yes."

"Did you find you a man inside? Because you damn sure don't act like you don't want any pussy." She walked away and he eyeballed her figure.

"Why did you threaten to kill Champagne?" he said.

She then turned and faced him. Her eyebrows were furled. "Is this what the bitch told you?"

"I know you did it."

"So what the fuck if I did? This bitch ain't no use to us. She's lucky I didn't kill her ass."

"Threatening her with pit bulls? Are you fuckin nuts?"

"You asked me to find the killers of your kids and I did what I thought I needed to do."

"Stop lying. You had her turning tricks before my kids even got murdered."

"That's all the bitch is good for!"

"I need you to stay away from that woman, okay? She's gone through enough."

"I do what the fuck I want." The sound of her Louboutins clacked on wooden floors as she walked toward the fridge. She got a bottle of white wine out, poured a glass, and sipped it.

"I got a lead on these Detroit boys."

"Okay. Let me know where they are at and I'll have someone take care of them," she said.

"I don't know where they are, but I know of somebody that might know them."

"Who is this person?"

"A stripper named Roxy."

"How do you know this?"

"Jailhouse talk."

TeTe raised her eyebrow skeptically. "Okay, who is this chick? Where does she work?"

"She used to work at the Pink Pony but I don't know where she's at now."

"So what am I supposed to do with this information if you don't know where she works now?"

"Can't you call John?"

"I can."

He stared at her for a while. He had to admit that he had missed her and he knew that she meant well. He pulled her close. She set the glass of wine down on the counter and he kissed her. "We are going to find these motherfuckers, and we're going to find them together."

"I love you."

"I love you too." She unbuckled his pants and dropped to her knees and sucked him until he exploded in her pretty little mouth, and she swallowed every drop of his seed.

● ● ●

Someone had run out of gas. A half-empty can was a few feet away from the car. Black sat on the trunk of a car, and Daniels sat on the hood of an SUV. They faced each other and were once again on a road just off Buford Highway. It was 44 degrees and Black was freezing his ass off. He sat on the trunk of the car, and the thin-ass windbreaker he wore could not suffice. Daniels stood with his hands inside his Levi pockets, nappy lumberjack beard blanketing his ashy face.

"I need you to help me find out where these motherfuckers are at. I need to find the motherfuckers that done this to my kids."

"I got you out for a reason."

"To help you make money. I know that, and I want to get paid, too, but you have to put yourself in my shoes."

"I get that you want revenge." Daniels licked his chapped lips.

The wind howled and Black covered his head with the hood of the jacket. "You don't get it." Black averted his gaze. "You don't get it at all, motherfucker. You still got your kids."

"And you have more," Daniels said. "Black, I'm working on something big, and if you hold tight I'll personally help you kill these dudes. The right way. Professionally, not some bullshit sloppy job that you'll spend the rest of your life in prison for. Understand?"

"Where is the work?"

"I don't have it yet. But if things go my way, you'll never have to do this shit again. Ever. It will be a one-time deal. You won't have to see me ever again; I don't ever have to see you."

"When is this going to happen?"

"I don't know yet."

"How do you know it's going to happen?"

Daniels raised an eyebrow and said, "I'm not going to get into the specifics. You'll hear about it."

Chapter 40

Terrell looked startled when Starr showed up at his house again. He was wearing Under Armour workout gear and was wiping his face with a towel when he invited her in.

She stepped inside and looked around. "Where is the trophy wife?"

"Jokes. Jokes. Jokes. You should have been a comedian. She hasn't been here."

Lies. Lies. Lies. You should have been an attorney.

He studied her face and body and could see a slight pudge in her stomach. "So you're going to keep it?"

"I don't know."

"How far are you along?"

"About nine weeks now.

"I tried calling you." He wiped his face with a towel.

"I had death in my family."

"I'm sorry to hear that." He half smiled.

"Would you like to take a seat?"

"I'm not going to be here long."

"What brings you here? You told me that you were going to kill the baby."

She frowned and said, "I never said anything like that."

He sat down and kicked his running shoes off, revealing black Under Armor ankle socks.

"What's on your mind?"

"I think I'm going to keep the baby."

He smiled. "I can kick the trophy wife to the curb and you and T.J. can move in with me. I would like that. I want a family."

"It's not quite that simple. I keep the baby, we co-parent, and you keep the trophy wife."

"So you're telling me that you're going to be with that dude...the hustler. The drug dealer."

"It's not what I'm saying at all."

"What are you saying?"

"I'm saying I changed my mind and we can co-parent the baby."

He disappeared into the kitchen and returned carrying a gallon of water. He chugged some down.

"Co-parent?"

"Co-parent." She sighed.

"What changed your mind?"

"My mind was never made up, one way or the other," Starr lied. She thought about how she'd been to the abortion clinic a few days earlier, but that was none of his goddamned business.

"I mean I don't want it to be like this, but what choice do I have in the matter?"

She looked at him and he looked defeated. "I'll make this as easy as possible. I won't be one of those baby mamas from hell. I won't take you to court for child support. You don't have to support it if you don't want. I make my own money. I'm not trying to get you for your money."

"Stop it." He chugged down half the gallon of water and said, "I know you don't want me for my money. I like the fact that you were working when I met you; this is precisely the reason I can't take the trophy wife serious. You still with the dope boy?"

"No," she lied, because she needed cooperation not resistance. If they were going to co-parent, she knew she couldn't lie about her relationship with Q forever.

"Okay, because I'm warning you, if you do decide to have the baby and you have that man around my child with some illegal shit, I'm filing for custody."

"What makes you think he's doing illegal shit?"

"Look, I'm from Chi-town. My whole family hustles. I know D-boys when I see them."

She stared at him and his eyes told her that he was serious about what he had said.

She half smiled. "The baby ain't even here yet, and it's already complicated."

"It's your fault. All you have to do is get rid of him and be with me."

"I'm not with anybody."

"Time will tell."

• • •

Black sat on the passenger side of Fresh's car. Fresh took a hit from the blunt and said, "You know I want to help you with anything you need." He took another long toke from the weed.

Black rolled his side window down to get some ventilation in the compact Porsche. The cold air smacked his face and he raised the window. Fresh passed him the blunt but he didn't take it. This was the third blunt. How could a motherfucker get sky high and still function?

Black looked Fresh in the eye and said, "I appreciate your concern, bruh, but I can handle this."

"I got dudes in Houston that will come up and kidnap these niggas."

Black said, "Can you dead this blunt right now?"

"Fresh stubbed the blunt out in an ashtray, losing it among a bunch of other half-smoked Swisher Sweets. "Did you think about what I asked?"

"I did."

"What do you want to do?"

"I don't want to do it. I don't need to do it. The last thing I need is a bunch of 'migos after my ass. I got shit I gotta do, bruh. I need to focus on this."

"I get it."

"Does Q know about this?"

"What do you mean?"

"Does he know what you're thinking? Does he know your plans?"

"Q is not my daddy."

"Not what I'm saying at all. I'm just thinking if you rob the plug, how is Q going to get more work?"

"Q has lots of connects. Plus, he'll be happy that this dude is gone."

Fresh drove to a neighborhood that Black had never seen. They drove until they were in a cul-de-sac. There was a huge cobblestone mansion on the right.

Black turned and said, "Where the fuck are we, bruh?"

"You're from Atlanta. You tell me." Fresh laughed.

Black said, "That means I'm supposed to know about every goddamned neighborhood in Atlanta?"

Fresh pointed at the house on the right and said, "That's the house."

Black frowned. The weed aroma still lingered. He lowered the window again and the hawk smacked him in the face again. He licked his dried his lips and raised the window. "Turn the heat on."

"We don't need the heat if you quit lowering the window."

"Why are we here?"

"That's the house."

"What house?"

"The house where the plug lives."

Black laughed and said, "You're determined to get me to do this."

Fresh said, "I just need your help, man. Please help me with this and I'll help you find the motherfuckers that killed your kids."

Black turned the heat up to sixty-seven. The hot air blew out of the vents on his side only. Black said, "Can I take care of my business first? Can I find the niggas that did this to my kids? Then I'll help you."

Chapter 41

Diego paced and wondered where the fuck was Q. Two henchman sat at the kitchen table playing Conquian, a Mexican card game similar to Rummy. A tall white Mexican named Paco, who had red hair and blue eyes, was there. He'd grown up in San Diego and moved to Texas when he was seventeen. He spoke perfect English when he said, "We don't need these niggas. I can do it all myself."

There was a long silence before one of the men looked up, nodded, and agreed. Diego called Q but didn't get an answer.

Paco said, "He doesn't respect you, Jefe. To him you're just another wetback. Kill him just like you did his friend. Fuck him and fuck Fresh."

Diego made his way over to where Paco stood. He was so close to him that he smelled tortillas on his breath. "I don't want to hear another word out of you."

"Jefe, I'm just saying—"

Diego grabbed him with one swift move then slammed Paco's head against the wall so hard, a picture frame across the room fell. Diego's elbow pressed against the man's neck and he was gasping for air. Diego wielded a knife and pierced his lips. Blood began leaking on Paco's t-shirt. "One more fucking word out of you and I will cut your tongue out. Is that understood?"

"Yes."

"Yes, what?"

"Yes, Jefe."

Diego released him and the phone rang. It was Q.

"Hello?" Diego put him on speakerphone so the rest of the men could hear.

"I'll be there in five minutes."

"Okay. I've been waiting."

"Sorry. I'm running late. Had something to take care of."

"Niggas are all ways late," Paco mumbled under his breath.

"See you in a few."

When he terminated the call, he gave Paco a look but didn't say anything. Ten minutes later, Q entered the house. Paco and the two men at the card table looked up and acknowledged Q.

"What's going on here? Y'all going to ambush me?"

Diego smiled. "No, of course not."

"I didn't know that you were going to have everybody and their mama here."

"Relax, Q, it's okay."

"I'm good."

Paco stared at Q but didn't say anything.

Diego said, "I got one thousand kilos right now. Did you bring a truck?"

"I can't take them right now."

Diego frowned. "What do you mean, you can't take them right now? What the hell am I going to do with this work? I had this shit brought up here especially for you, and I didn't give Fresh shit because you told me not to give him shit. Now you tell me you're not going to take it."

"I'm going to take it."

"When?"

Q made eye contact with Diego and said, "I have to find a place to store it."

"You have to find a place to store it? Use the same place that you stored it when you got it from Gordo."

"Look, I'll be back," Q said.

Paco laughed and said something slick in Spanish, but Q understood what the word 'puta' meant.

Q turned to him. "What, motherfucker?"

Then he grabbed Paco and slammed him to the floor. Miguel, one of the other henchmen, stood up from the card game and grabbed Q.

Diego slapped the shit out of Paco and kicked him. "Apologize to Q!"

Q broke free from Miguel's grip and said, "I'll be back in a day or two. But next time it's just me and you."

• • •

Gordo's well-done ribs were still sizzling on the plate. Q sat across from his friend at Houston's as Gordo feasted like he hadn't eaten in days. Gordo was a man who enjoyed food and the finer things in life. After a few glasses of sweet tea, the blonde waitress had left the pitcher in the middle of the table. Gordo poured another glass of tea. He squeezed lemons into the glass and then said, "The job has to be done right, but it can't look like it had anything to do with our team."

The man known as Salsa said, "It's going to be a clean job, boss."

"It has to be a clean job, understand? Because if word gets back to my uncle, he'll want to kill us all."

Q and Gordo struck up a side conversation. Q said, "So you're really going to go through with it?"

Gordo said to Q, "We're like brothers. Brothers to the end. Not only do I want my cousin dead, I want to take over his business."

"So killing him is beneficial to you too."

"It's the cost of doing business, my friend."

Q couldn't understand the logic of that. He had grown up dirt-poor, but the thought of killing a family member for business was something he didn't think he could ever do.

Gordo diced the steak into smaller pieces. He smiled and gave a thumbs up. The steak was perfect.

"How many people was in the house?"

"There were three."

"Three?"

"Yes."

"No kids?"

"No kids."

Gordo said, "This is what I want you to do…"

Q listened closely. He poured a glass of tea and gulped it but spat it out. It tasted like syrup and water.

"Call him and tell him you're coming to get the work."

"It's probably gone by now."

"Tell them that the stash house is right down the road and that you need him to meet you there alone."

"But then what is going to happen?"

"I'll show up."

"What do you think he's going to say?"

"He's going to be a little puzzled at first, but he'll open the door. I'm his cousin. We'll kill him and all of his men."

Q bit his fingernails.

Gordo said, "Don't worry, my friend. This won't come back on you."

Chapter 42

F by Ferragamo Black made Jada want to take her panties off. It was a cheap cologne but, man, did it have an effect on her. Tank stood in her living room smelling heavenly, dressed in casual but expensive wear. He'd showed up unannounced and that had pissed her the fuck off. Fresh had done it before, but that was Fresh. And although she liked Tank, they weren't on that level. He was married. She had to admit that the motherfucker smelled good, and damn he was fine. Arms all buffed like he'd just left the gym.

"Showing up unannounced will get your ass expelled from the Queendom," Jada said.

"I called you and you didn't answer."

Jada looked at him, thinking, Okay, this motherfucker wants to play mind games. He had called her one time and she didn't answer. One time, but now that's supposed to translate to he's been calling her? She knew the real reason he had only called once is because he had to spend time with that ho.

Jada played along with his silly ass. "Oh, you called me? I don't have a missed call on my phone. How many times did you call me?"

"At least six times."

"Damn, that's odd. I guess your calls are the only ones that didn't go through. You might want to get your phone checked out."

"You got jokes?"

"No, you got jokes, motherfucker, knowing damn well you ain't call me." She smiled. "I understand that you gotta spend time with Country?"

"Who?"

"Your chick. How many times I gotta tell you that I'm calling your girl Country?"

"You're a funny chick."

"You think I like to play games?"

"I didn't say that. So what's been up? You been with your boy, I guess."

"What I do is none of your fucking business."

He smiled, and though his smile was beautiful, it was annoying the hell out of her.

"So what did you come here for, Tank?"

"I came to check up on you." He walked slowly, looking around as if he were looking for a clue.

The house cleaner had just left, so he could search the motherfucker top to bottom for all she cared.

"He's been here?"

She put her hands on her hips and said, "And if he has?"

"That's a yes."

"Why are you here, Tank?"

He looked at her like he was surprised, studying her face and wondering why her demeanor had changed. He reasoned that she was certainly fucking Fresh again. He could just feel it. "You're right, Jada. I have no reason to come in here looking around asking questions."

"You don't, and to answer your question: I have been with Fresh."

"I know."

"How do you know?"

"I can just tell." He paused. "I don't blame you. "I'm not stepping up and letting my intentions be known."

She looked at him. I'm having fun like you're having fun.

But I do want to find a man and settle down."

"Jada, the reason why you really haven't heard from me is that I was in San Francisco."

"What's in San Francisco?"

"I sell weed."

"Okay. Tell me something I didn't know."

"Jada, come on. You didn't know I sold weed."

"I knew you sold something."

"Yeah, I remember you asking me that. Kind of hinting at it."

"That's what I attract. I attract drug dealers. I've fucked a few professional men. Doctors, attorneys, a couple of athletes; but for the most part it's been hustlers."

"I didn't want to tell you what I was into."

"Because you didn't know me."

"Right."

"Tank, what do you want from me? How can I help you?"

"I want you and I don't want you to be with nobody else. I don't want you to be with Fresh. I told you that, and just to know that you have been with him kills me inside."

She laughed and said, "It kills you inside, huh? I'm just curious to know how it kills you inside when you disappear for a few days and I don't hear from you?" She sat on the armchair in her living room and then chuckled. "Then, you come with some bullshit about you been blowing my phone up, knowing damn well your ass ain't called."

"I'm sorry."

"What are you sorry for?"

"I'm sorry for lying."

"You don't get it. You're sorry for lying but you're not sorry for neglecting me."

"I neglected you?"

"I need attention. I have daddy issues, but it's not your fault."

"I don't want you with him."

"If you don't want me to be with him, leave her and be with me. I'm grown. I need more if I am going to fully commit to anyone."

He stared at her as his cologne lingered in the air. The way he looked at her, she could tell that he wanted her.

"Cut her off and come get me if you want me."

"I can't do it just yet."

"Why not? Is she pregnant?"

Silence. He finally sighed. "Yeah, she's pregnant and I've been trying to get her to abort the baby! She don't want to do it. Giving me all that 'It's a blessing from God' bullshit."

Jada just stared without responding.

"Why are you looking at me like that?"

"Tank, go home and be with your family."

Chapter 43

Sirens were getting closer but no police car was in view yet.

Fy-Head told her obese friend named Denise to floor the Camaro while lowering the radio and the window. Inside the trunk were several thousand dollars' worth of stolen merchandise: laptop computers, cameras, clothing, shoes. She and Denise had been shoplifting for the past couple of days, and everything had been going well until one nosey-ass cracker had tried to stop them in Walmart, asking to search her bag.

"Hell no, you can't search my bag. Why the fuck are you racial profiling me?" Fy-Head had proclaimed, but of course there had been no racial profiling. Security had actually seen her stuff some lingerie in her crotch and inside her handbag.

Inside the bag was costume jewelry. She had slapped the old cracker with the bag and bolted to the Camaro, and now they were on I-285 trying to beat the all-points-bulletin for a cherry red Camaro with tinted windows. No license plate number. Fy-Head had ripped the tag off before entering Wal-Mart. But a bright red Camaro wouldn't be hard to spot. Only now that they were on the run did she think it was a bad idea to drive a red car.

"I need you to speed yo ass up."

"I'm going as fast as I can."

"Go faster."

"I can't."

Fy-Head looked behind and she could see a police cruiser in view now. And now there was a helicopter trailing them. "Damn, I'm going to jail. I'm a fucking habitual offender. I'm going back to prison all because of yo slow ass."

"What? I can't believe you're saying that."

Fy-Head looked back and said, "I'm sorry. I'm going to need you to pull over and then I'm going to hop out and run."

"We're on the highway. I can't just pull over and stop and let you hop out and run. What about me?"

"I'm going to get the shit out the trunk and run."

"Bad idea."

"Cut across the damn median then," Fy-Head said.

Denise drove the car across the median and a Honda Pilot crashed into the passenger side. They fish-tailed and spun all the way around, now traveling in the opposite direction of the traffic, zig-zagging to avoid the oncoming cars. An eighteen-wheeler was headed in their direction, so Fy-Head grabbed the steering wheel.

"Bitch, you're trying to kill us!"

"I'm trying to get away like you said."

The car was crossing the median when the tire exploded.

"Fuck!" Fy-Head said. "Keep driving."

"On the rims?

"Hell yeah!"

Denise tried to drive the car on the rim but couldn't get traction.

Fy-Head hopped out the car and made a run for it.

A young, white state trooper with a Mohawk parked his car and ran after her. He tackled her before she could disappear into the woods.

Denise was surrounded.

Fy-Head wrestled with the trooper and was putting up a good fight until the man removed a device from his waist and tasered the fuck out of her. She hollered like a wounded animal.

She lay on her face, handcuffed.

A car full of teens drove by and pulled out their cameras. They snapchatted the whole thing.

Chapter 44

Black lay in TeTe's bed staring up at the spinning ceiling fan, thinking about his babies. Did they beg and plead before they were murdered? Did they suffer? He had hoped that they died right away, no suffering. He was still upset with himself that he didn't even get to give them the proper good-bye. He knew they had to be in heaven—they were kids. Perhaps they were in heaven with Lani, all looking down on him. He smiled then his phone rang. He looked at his clock. It was 2.45 a.m. Who could be calling him at this time? He picked up the phone.

Daniels.

He sent him to voicemail but Daniels called again and again and finally Black picked up the phone. "What the fuck do you want?"

"You're about to be one rich motherfucker."

"What are you talking about?"

"I need you to meet me. Meet me right away."

"Now?"

"Yes, now, and bring a truck."

"Where the hell am I going to get a truck this time of night?"

"I don't know. Find one."
"Give me two hours."
"Okay."

● ● ●

Black had borrowed a truck from his daddy. Well, he stole it. He took the keys from Bo, who was asleep, and left a note that said he was going to bring the truck back in the morning. He knew that Bo would be up in a few hours. He usually started his day around 6:30. He had hoped by that time he would be on his way back.

He met Daniels at their usual pick-up location, the run-down warehouse.

Daniels appeared smiling and Black said, "What the hell is going on?"

"I'm about to make you a rich man."

"I'm listening."

"What can you do with one thousand kilos?"

"Kilos of what?"

"Coke."

"Are you serious?"

"Yes. Very serious."

"I don't know. I've never had that much in my life."

Daniels said, turn your truck around and back it up.

Black backed his truck up to the dock then hopped out and ran around back to help Daniels load the truck. The product was in big green duffle bags. Daniels removed a kilo from one of the bags and said, "This shit is raw; you can cut it a few times."

"No need for all that."

"Why is it green?"

"I don't know. Sometimes things are like that. I seen it looking all kinds of ways."

"How long is it going to take to get rid of this?" Daniels asked.

"What's the split?"

"50/50."

Black did the calculations in his head—a thousand kilos at

$28,000. That was twenty-eight million dollars, and half of that was fourteen million. Damn, he was going to be set. Shamari would be good when he got out, and there would be no need to hustle. He could buy more Wings Kings. Maybe a Papa John's. Get closer with his older kids and retire.

"So when do you think you going to have the money?"

"You asked me this already."

"What's your answer?"

"I don't know."

"I need my part of the money in one month. I can't wait longer than a month."

"Okay."

Black's phone rang. His father. "Hello."

"Hello, my ass. Bring me my goddamn truck!"

"I'm on my way."

Chapter 45

Fy-Head had asked to go into protective custody because of the last time she'd been in the county jail. She thought that if she went into general population, she would be safe because of her HIV status. But instead, she had been brutally raped and gang-banged night after night.

When she had complained to staff, they told her that she should have asked for PC earlier. She eventually had to get her attorney to have her moved into PC, but this time it would be a different story. Because of what they had on file about her, she was sent to PC right away.

PC consisted mostly of child molesters, snitches, and trannies. She had chosen to stay in her room for the first three days. She and another tranny named Diamond Princess were roommates. She thought she would see her friend Denise, but her record wasn't as bad and so she had bailed out days ago.

During the three days that she had been in her cell, she had read hood novel after hood novel, and she was tired of reading those ghetto-ass stories. She decided to go out into the common area to watch TV, and that's when she saw him sitting there on the table watching the news.

Dr. Craig Matthews. The man who had murdered his wife. The monster that had murdered Fy-Head's best friend. The man that was responsible for a number of voluptuous asses. It took every ounce of strength in her body not to run up and smack the fuck out of him. She knew that if she fought him, she would easily whoop his ass. But if she whopped his ass, there was a chance that an asshole LT. would throw her in GenPop, to the wolves, twenty-four-hour ass-draggings and gang rapes.

She approached him. He had the remote control in his hand flicking through channels. "Hey, it's two o'clock; do you mind if I watch the soaps?"

He kept flicking the channels without looking her way. "What channel?"

"Channel nine. The Young and the Restless."

He turned to offer her the remote. Their eyes locked and held. He stared at her for a very long time without saying a word. But then he said, "What are you doing here?"

"When you do something wrong, they put you in jail. I'm sure you know all about doing wrong, Dr. Matthews."

"Can I speak to you in private?"

She laughed and said, "We're in jail. There is no privacy in here; you know that."

He set the remote down on the table then hopped up. She followed him to another table and sat beside him. "Why did you have to kill her?"

"I didn't mean for her to die."

"You shot her."

"I didn't shoot her."

"You fuckin liar. I will kick yo punk ass right now."

"I didn't plan for her to die. I was looking for you. You know I was looking for you. You stole my money and I thought she knew where you was."

A creepy-looking dude with unkempt dreadlocks stood behind her and lusted after her manufactured ass.

Craig said, "Can you let us have a moment?"

The man stood there grinning, rubbing his hands together.

Fy-Head turned and said, "My status is HIV positive."

The man frowned and walked away.

Fy-Head said, "You killed my best friend."

"I didn't mean for her to die. All you had to do was give me my money. You cheated me out of ten grand."

"I'm sorry about that."

"And I'm sorry about what happened to your friend."

They were both silent. They needed each other. They needed to form a truce. Neither of them wanted to go into GenPop.

"I know you want to kill me. But what's that going to solve?"

Fy-Head sighed and said, "I forgive you."

"If you need anything, I have plenty of commissary."

Fy-Head said, "I don't need shit right now, but I'll let you know." She moved to the next table. The Young and the Restless was on.

•   •   •

Q had called Diego six times in the last two days but got no answer. Gordo and his men were waiting to get the word so that he could send the men over to take his cousin out. He had to eliminate the competition and takeover Atlanta. This would get rid of a terrible human being, as far as Gordo was concerned.

Q said to Gordo, "He's not answering."

"You should just go over there. You know where he lives."

"Why don't you call your uncle to find out if he's heard anything from him?"

"I called him already. He said that he hasn't heard from him since the shipment."

"Do you think he's in jail?"

"No."

"How can you be so sure?"

"He would have called someone."

"I'll go over."

"Call me as soon as you hear something. We're still in town."

Chapter 46

When Q pulled up to Diego's house, all the cars that he'd seen days before were still in the driveway. He rang the bell. No answer.

He rang it again and still no answer. He cocked his weapon before running around back. The back door was slightly open and a stench was coming from the house. He decided he would walk in. His gun in hand, ready for action, just in case someone fired a shot at him. He eased through the kitchen and that's when he spotted blood on kitchen tile and a bloody kitchen counter right underneath the microwave.

He kept walking. "Diego?"

No answer.

He walked with his gun drawn, and when he entered the living room from the kitchen, that's when he saw the first body sprawled across floor. The dead man's wife beater was beet red like he'd been stabbed at least twenty times. Q hopped over the body and entered the main bedroom. Then he spotted Diego lying across the bed with multiple gunshot wounds to the back of the head. The final body was in the bathroom with a slit throat.

Q called Gordo.

"Hello."

"Get over here."

"What's going on?"

"You ain't going to believe this shit."

"What?"

"Diego is dead."

"What?"

"He's been murdered along with the three other dudes."

"Get out of there, Q. Leave and we'll call the police. Don't touch shit. Just leave."

"I can't just leave here."

"This is going to be a drug-related investigation. You can't make yourself a target."

"You're right."

"Leave now and get a new phone. I will meet you where I spoke to you last."

"I understand."

• • •

Q found out where Terrell lived, so he drove to his house and rang the doorbell. Terrell's girlfriend opened the door and Q said, "I'm here to see Terrell."

"Is he expecting you?"

"Yes," he lied. Q examined the young woman's body and was quite impressed with Terrell's taste. It was good he had someone because Starr was off limits. The woman disappeared and ran upstairs.

Seconds later, Terrell came running downstairs dressed in a T-shirt and long shorts. When he spotted Q, he said, "What the fuck are you doing showing up at my goddamn house?"

"Honey, do you want me to call the police?" his girlfriend asked.

"Can we talk for a minute?"

Terrell looked at his woman then back at Q and said, "It's okay. Let me talk to him for a second."

"I'll go upstairs."

"No, you don't have to. I'll talk to him outside."

Terrell stepped outside and Q said, "Nice-looking chick

you got there, and she has a fat ass." He paused and said, "Is it real?"

"What?"

"Is her ass real? You gotta ask these days."

"What the fuck are you doing here?"

"I'm just going to get down to business." He turned to the vehicles that were parked in the driveway. "You have a nice car, nice house, nice girl with a nice little fake ass. You've built a nice life for yourself."

"And?"

"Don't you want to keep it?"

"Keep what?"

"Keep living, motherfucker!"

"What the hell are you talking about?"

"I'm going to need you to stay away from Starr."

"I've already spoken with Starr. She told me that she is going to keep the baby and we're going to co-parent."

"I heard there was a threat made."

"What are you talking about?"

"You said if she brings your child around a drug dealer boyfriend, you're going to take her to court to get custody."

"I said that and it's true."

"Well you made your threat and now it's time for me to make my threat."

Terrell huffed and said, "I ain't got time for your shit, bruh."

"What?" Q removed a .45 handgun from his waist and said, "Oh, but you do have time. You don't have nothing but time. Now step aside so I can go break the news to your little bitch that you're going to be a father."

"I was just kidding. I would never go try to take custody from Starr."

Q said, "You need to stay the fuck away from Starr or else I'll kill you. Do you understand? You're the basketball player, and I'm the gangster."

"I got you, bruh."

Chapter 47

Jada called Tank but his phone went to voice mail. She called Fresh and he picked up right away.

"I need a fix."

"I could use a fix too. It's been a fucked up week."

"What's wrong, babe?"

"I get like this when I ain't making money."

"You coming over?"

"On my way."

Fresh arrived thirty minutes later and Jada was wearing a sexy nightgown.

"When was the last time you seen Black?" he asked.

"A couple of days ago."

"Yeah? I've been trying to reach him."

"He came over and left some money for Shamari."

"How much money are they allowed to have in there?"

"Well this money is for when he get out. He wanted me to put it up."

"How much did he leave?"

Jada raised her eyebrows and said, "You're getting a little nosy, ain't you?"

"I was just asking a question, boo." He slapped her ass.

"Well if you must know, it was a couple of hundred thousand."

"What?"

"Yeah."

Fresh paced and then said, "Jada, I'm going to tell you something that I don't want to get back to Black."

"What?"

"A couple of days ago I showed Black where my plug lived. I asked him to get a team together and rob the dude."

Jada said, "Shiesty."

"Not really. This dude killed a guy that was like an uncle to me. Cut me off for no reason, so I was going to get him back, you feel me?"

Jada still looked at his ass with the side eye. He was Q's friend and Q had plotted to kill Trey. They were just alike, if you asked her. "Okay. So you take him by the connect's house and ask him to rob the connect?"

"Yeah."

"And what happened?"

"He says he's not going to do it. Has to find the dude that killed his kids."

"And I understand that."

"But now you telling me he dropped off a couple of hundred thousand dollars?"

"You think he did it?"

"The connect was murdered. What do you think?"

"Damn. If he did, that was fucked up."

● ● ●

Jada telephoned Black and told him she needed to meet him right away. They decided to meet at Hickory Tavern. They both ordered drinks. When they arrived, she sipped her drink and said, "I'm going to need you to be honest with me, Black."

"Jada, I'm a new man."

"Really?"

He sipped his drink and said, "All that lying and taking crazy chances, putting my family and friends at risk. That's over. I have to get these clowns for what they did to my family, and after that I'm done with this shit."

"I get all of that."

His eyes were serious. "So what's up?"

"Did you rob Fresh's connect?"

"You can't be serious?"

She kept a straight face and he knew that she was serious.

"Did Fresh tell you this?"

"Answer the question, Black. Did you or didn't you do it?"

"I swear to God I didn't do that. Jada, where the fuck is this coming from?"

"Black, me and you go back a long time. You were my best friend's so-called man at one time, so on the strength of her, I'll protect you."

"I didn't do shit. I would tell you if I did that." Black gulped down his drink and flagged the waitress. He ordered another double then gulped it down.

"Black, the connect got robbed and murdered."

Black slammed his fist hard on the table and said, "What the fuck does that have to do with me?"

"Nothing. I'm just asking, my brother."

There was a long silence. Black avoided Jada's eyes then finally he said, "I can't believe you asked me some shit like that."

"Black, all I know is that you come over my house telling me that you're set. Telling me Mari is set when he get out, and gave me a couple hundred thousand dollars."

"And?"

"And Fresh told me that a few days ago you and him drove by the connect's house, and he wanted you to do a job for him—rob the connect."

"That did happen, but I told him I had to handle my business; you know I had two children that got murdered."

"I know that."

"He asked me to do something that I wasn't willing to do right now."

"Where did you suddenly come up with money to put aside for Shamari?"

"Jada, I've always had money. I may not have the kind

of money that Fresh and Q has, but you know that I'm a hustler."

"I know. But just think about how that must look: you drop off two hundred grand over here for Mari, and Fresh's connect got robbed and murdered after he shows you where the man lives."

"Jada, look at me. I didn't rob the man, and I ain't murder nobody."

"Did you follow the connect before and ask him to deal with you?"

"That was a long time ago. I didn't rob the man's connect."

"Where did you get the money for me to put aside for Mari?"

"Is Fresh trying to take that money from you?"

"Nobody is trying to take shit from me."

"Good because it didn't come from his connect."

"Where did the money come from?"

"The streets is all I'm going to say." Black stood and tossed a hundred-dollar bill on the table and looked at Jada. "I don't like being interrogated."

Chapter 48

Black met Daniels at the spot again and Black handed him two Samsonite suitcases with six million in cash. Daniels loaded the money into the back of his pickup truck and then lit a cigarette. He opened the door of the truck and sat down in the driver's seat, leaving the door open.

Black stood in front of him. "Bruh, who did you take this shit from?"

"What difference does it make? You're going to have more money than you will ever have in your life when I'm done."

"Did you hear about the four Mexicans who got murdered?"

"I'm an FBI agent; you know I've heard about it."

"Did you do it?"

"Did I do what?"

"Murder them and take their shit."

"What did the news say?"

"The news said they believed it was a drug-related robbery."

"Then that's what it was."

"What do you think?"

"I think you need to quit asking so many goddamn questions."

Black watched him carefully. "You followed Fresh to his

house and found out about Diego and robbed him and killed him."

"You're smart, Black, a little too damn smart."

"Motherfucker, now these dudes think I had something to do with this shit. I was the only one that was from Atlanta that knew where they lived."

"I'll protect you."

"I don't need protection. I need to get the fuck away from you."

"Do you want to go back to jail?"

"What?"

"I'm the one that got you out of jail. All I have to do is say I'm done with your ass and they'll lock you up for sure."

"You threatening me?"

"Take it the way you want to take it."

Black sighed and said, "Bruh, you should have told me that this is what you were going to do."

"You have more dope than you've ever seen in your life. You sell this shit and you can get out of the game. I thought that's what the goal was. The goal of every dope boy is to one day get out of the game, Black. I'm not stupid. You sell this shit and you get about ten million on the street. You know how much I get? Two million dollars. You are making more than me."

"How?"

"I have to split this shit with my compadres."

"Fuck that. Don't try to change the subject. Motherfucker, do you know that you can get my ass killed?"

"They're not going to kill you."

"How do you know?"

"Nobody gave a damn about this Diego dude."

"I just wish you would have told me."

"Black, finish selling this product and then you don't ever have to see me again."

"Somehow I believe that's a lie."

•   •   •

The two men trailed the woman driving the Telsa, a little

girl on the passenger side. One of the men named Blue was on the phone receiving his orders.

"I need you to pull up on the car and start dumping rounds into it," the voice on the other end of the phone said.

"I can't shoot the car up. There is a little girl. I'm not going to shoot a little girl. I'm sorry but that's just not in my makeup," Blue said.

The driver was a guy named Big Keith, who was from New York, and they'd called him Big Keith ever since he was thirteen years old. He had been the biggest kid in the neighborhood, a stout guy with a massive stomach.

Keith said, "You drive and I'll shoot the motherfucker up. I don't have time for this sympathy shit."

Blue said, "Keith, will you just shut the fuck up?"

"Let Keith drive. I want this job done and I want it done right now."

"I'm going to do the job because I want to do it right."

The Tesla got between a tractor trailer and a Volvo.

Keith said, "I'll pull up beside the car and just shoot the bitch. The little girl don't have to get hit."

"But the little girl still dies. You think she's going to live if the driver is dead?"

"I don't give a fuck about who lives and who dies. They didn't give a damn about who lived when my brother had to die. Do the job!"

"We just killed two kids a few weeks ago, and I'm not killing another kid," Blue said. "I can still picture that little girl begging for her life. That shit fucks with me."

The Tesla pulled off the exit and drove into a gated neighborhood. Big Keith followed them until he was stopped at the gate by security.

"I'm with her."

The man just waved them through. Big Keith tailed the Tesla to a house at the end of the road. The little girl hopped out of the car and ran into the arms of a Hispanic woman as the Tesla pulled off again. It cruised past the guard station and hoped back on the Interstate.

Big Keith punched the ignition and pulled alongside the Tesla. Blue hung out the window and dumped sixteen shots into the side of the car. The woman slumped in the car, and the Tesla crossed the median and met an oncoming eighteen-wheeler that made quick work of the vehicle.

Blue said to Big Keith, "You satisfied?"

"I would've even killed the little bitch."

Chapter 49

Starr had spent the night with Q. She had showered, brushed her teeth, and kissed Q goodbye. When she opened the door to leave, there were two police officers standing in front of her. The tall black man with the thick mustache said, "I'm looking for Quentin Mills."

Q entered the living room and saw the officers questioning Starr. "What's going on?"

"Are you Quentin Mills?"

"Yes."

"Mr. Mills, you're under arrest for communicating a threat."

"What? Who did I threaten?"

"Mr. Mills, can you put your hands behind your back?"

Starr said, "Wait a minute. Who did he threaten?"

"He'll find out when he gets downtown."

"You can't tell me who I threatened, then I ain't doing shit!"

The officer said, "Sir, just put your hands behind your back. I will give you a copy of the warrant once I get you in the car."

"How the hell am I going to read the warrant with my hands

behind my back?"

"Are you refusing to cooperate?"

"Fuck you."

The two officers moved in on Q. Starr was behind one of the officers who turned and said, "Ma'am, don't make us lock you up." He pushed her.

"Don't touch me."

Q said, "Don't touch my goddamn girlfriend. She's pregnant."

The man said to Q, "Communicating a threat is a small charge; you can get right out. It's not a big deal. Don't make this a bigger deal than it already is."

Starr said, "He's right."

Q said, "I apologize but, damn, all of my neighbors are going to see me get arrested."

The tall black officer said, "Listen, man, since you cooperated, I'll let you drive yourself downtown and we'll follow."

"Oh yeah? Are you serious?"

"Yes."

Starr said, "I'll take you."

"Can I see the warrant?"

The cop was pissed, but he passed him a copy of the warrant. The warrant made it clear that Quentin Mills, a.k.a Q, did intentionally and willfully threaten to kill Terrell...

Starr looked at him and shook her head. It was all there.

"I can explain."

"Tell me about it in the car."

• • •

Fresh was startled when Black rang his bell. He invited him in without speaking or offering him a seat.

Black stood in the doorway trying to think of how he was going to start the conversation. Black said, "I heard your plug got robbed and murdered, and I'm just here to let you know that it wasn't me. I ain't have shit to do with it."

Fresh eyed Black and he had to give him credit. The nigga sounded convincing.

"You don't believe me?"

"It's not about whether I believe you or not; it's about whether they believe you."

"Who is they?"

"The Alvarez cartel."

"What are you saying, bruh?"

"I expect to see the plug's uncle in a few days, and you know that he's going to think I had something to do with it. You know why?"

"Because you're the one that was dealing with him in Atlanta."

"That, and because I'm a nigga. You know they don't trust niggas. But they have to deal with niggas because we're in the streets. So right now it looks like I did it, or had something to do with it."

"I get that."

"Do you?"

"I know it looks fucked up, bruh. I know it, but on my dead kids I didn't kill your plug, bruh."

"You're the only one that knew where they lived except me and Q."

"How do you know that they weren't dealing with someone else?"

"Because I know."

Black laughed and said, "Wait a minute, partner. You took me over there a few days ago. You wanted me to rob this motherfucker, remember?"

"I got a great memory."

"Okay. If I robbed him, then it was going to come back on you."

"The difference is, somebody—and you said that somebody ain't you—robbed them and I didn't get a damn thing from it. I would have taken the chance of the shit falling on me if I was going to get something out of the deal." Fresh paused and said, "I ain't get shit out of the deal. All I know is that you're in the position to give your man, who's locked up, two hundred grand, and the connect is dead. Murdered."

Black chuckled, not because it was funny but because he couldn't believe this was happening to him.

"It's funny?" Fresh grabbed Black by the collar and slammed him against the wall.

Black pushed him off, grabbed a gun from his waist, and aimed it at Fresh's head. "Don't make me use this, motherfucker. The last time you pulled your gun on me I let that shit slide because I was wrong for hollering at the connect. But this time I'm not; I didn't do shit wrong."

Fresh threw his hands up.

Black's eyes did not blink. "Do you think I would have came here if I really had something to do with this shit?"

Silence.

"You are looking at a man that ain't got shit to lose. Try me if you want to, nigga!"

Fresh said, "Get the fuck out my house."

Black backed out of the house, gun still pointed it Fresh.

Chapter 50

Black had received a call from Champagne. She had him meet her right away at a local restaurant over drinks.

"I know where two of those Detroit boys are at."

"Where? And how do you know?" Black studied her face and there were a million thoughts running though his mind. How did she know where they were, and when did she learn this information? What would he do if he saw them? How was he going to kill them?

"They are staying out in Alpharetta."

"How do you know?"

"You remember the girl I was telling you about?"

"The one you said had gone back to Memphis?"

"Yeah, her."

"What about her?"

Well, she's back and we worked together the other night at the club, and you know I complimented her on her outfit, purposely trying to get next to her. She said she had somebody for me to meet and it turned out to be a friend of one of the Detroit boys. They took me out to a house out in Alpharetta and that's where I saw them."

"You saw them?"

"Blowed trees with them and chilled while watching the Pistons game. Niggas are Pistons fanatics."

"Sorry-ass Pistons."

"They from Detroit, remember?"

Black trembled. He knew that he was going to kill these motherfuckers. It was just a matter of how.

"Do you want me to show you the house?"

"You don't have to do that. Do you have the address?"

"I do."

"Text it to me."

"So where is your pit bull?"

"Huh?"

"Your old-ass girlfriend."

"I don't know. Haven't spoken to her."

"You know, Black, what that bitch did to me wasn't right. You need to check her."

"I've already handled the situation."

"I love you, Black."

He looked at her oddly.

She laughed and said, "Not that way. I like you more in a big brother kind of way. Even though we've fucked a couple of times. I can't explain how I feel for you."

"I think I understand."

"You know you always have looked out for me. Always have done things for me. Not always wanting ass for what you've done."

"I like you too. But why are you telling me all of this?"

"I'm sure you're going to kill these clowns that did this to your kids."

"I am."

"I think I'm leaving the game. You know, the stripper business. I'm going to the Lou. I can't take this shit. I've been dancing for a long time, and it's not getting me anywhere."

"I can dig that. I feel that way about hustling."

Silence.

"Take care of yourself, Black."

"When you leaving?"

"I'm leaving this weekend."

He stood and hugged her. Grabbed her ass.

And she smacked him playfully.

"Keep in touch."

"For sure."

"Follow me on Snapchat."

"I don't fuck with social media. What kind of gangster would I be?"

"You need to chill out, Black. Don't get lost in these streets."

He hugged her again and grabbed her ass. "I just had to get one more squeeze."

"You're a mess, Black."

• • •

Starr bailed Q out of jail at 2:20 in the morning and waited on him in the parking lot across from the jail. T.J. was asleep in the backseat.

Q finally climbed into the passenger side then he leaned forward to kiss her.

She dodged his kiss then turned to him and said, "Do you want to tell me what this was all about?"

"Did you read the warrant?"

"Yes."

"Well, you know what it was about."

"Look, motherfucker, you asked me to bail you out of jail, not the other way around."

"I'm sorry."

"What happened?"

"I just thought life would be easier if this motherfucker wasn't around. Like all the way out of the picture."

"You threatened to kill him? Not only did you threaten to kill him, you show up at his house. Who are you, man?"

"You can't imagine how violated I feel right now. My lady has another man's seed inside her."

"And you were the one that said you could deal with it."

"I did and I can, but do you know how this shit is going to feel if you have to co-parent with him?"

"Women do this shit all the time. Niggas go out here and cheat and then have a baby on the side and expect the woman to deal with it. My mama had to deal with it. But in my case, I didn't cheat."

"Because we were on a break."

"No, because we were on a break and you decided to run around with bitches."

They rode in silence for a few moments then he said, "I'm sorry."

Starr said, "You see, Trey, this bothers me."

"Trey?"

"Q. I meant Q, but Trey is on my mind. The fact that you were going to kill Trey still haunts me because I don't know who the fuck you are anymore."

"I'm me. Q."

"A cold-blooded killer."

"Don't give me that shit. You knew what kind of nigga I was from day one. I ain'tget this far being nice."

"You're a liar, a fucking liar."

"I'm not a liar."

"Can you deal with raising another man's kid or not?"

"I can."

"Well shut the fuck up then. It's almost three in the morning; I don't wanna hear this shit."

Chapter 51

The smell of bacon was in the air as Fresh and Q chomped down breakfast on the terrace. Eggs whites, bacon, and orange juice. "I got a call from Diego's uncle last night and he's not happy about what happened to Diego." Q said.

"Who gives a fuck?"

"You should."

"Why should I?"

"He think you had Diego killed."

"What?"

"Come on, Fresh, you knew that was coming. You were the only one in ATL dealing with him."

"So now what? What are they going to do, try to kill me?"

"No. I'm not going to let that happen."

"Just like you didn't let that happened to Rico, right?"

Q spread butter on his toast and then said, "Don't worry about it. Nothing is going to happen to you. They need us more than ever."

"I know who killed him."

"What? How do you know?"

Fresh avoided Q's stare, dropped a slice of bacon in his mouth and said, "It was Black."

"Black don't even know Diego."

"A few months ago, me and Diego was out having lunch and Black approached the table and introduced himself. Later, I found out that Black had followed Diego to a gas station and tried to get him to deal with him."

"Snake-ass Atlanta nigga."

"Yeah."

"Diego told you this?"

"Yes."

"I don't get it. So Diego wasn't dealing with him?"

"I don't think so."

"But how did he know where Diego lived?"

"I showed him. I asked him to rob him, but he said that he couldn't and wouldn't."

"So how do you know it was him that did it?"

"He was murdered a few days later. A few days after I told him about Diego."

That don't mean shit, Q thought, as he remembered how he too had plotted to kill Diego.

"I was with Jada the other day and she said that Black had come over and left two hundred thousand dollars for Shamari."

"Who the fuck is Shamari?"

"Jada's ex. He's supposed to be getting out soon. I guess"

"Black has money."

"Black don't have that kind of money to be giving somebody two hundred grand."

"So he did it?"

"I'm sure."

"We have to kill him."

"I don't want to."

"The Mexicans are going to kill you if we don't kill somebody."

"Fuck them Mexicans. I don't give a fuck about them. I'm not killing a nigga because a wetback died. Do I have to keep reminding you that these are the same motherfuckers that killed our homie?"

"You are the one that did business with Diego."

"And the plan was for him to die. He's dead."

"And they think you did it."

Fresh guzzled some OJ and then said, "They were going to think that anyway."

"But you ain't get not one dime. How many kilos do you think he had? At least a thousand, and Black didn't give you shit."

Fresh seethed underneath his breath.

• • •

Champagne's last night at the club was bittersweet. She was happy that she'd made thirty-five hundred dollars, but she was sad that this was the last night she would see her girls. Her best friends that she had made in Atlanta. Malicious and Shawty Red, both Atlanta girls, she had known since she'd moved from St Louis. The three girls were besties.

Shawty Red was a thick woman with a skinny waist and a tattoo of a Butterfly on her ass cheeks. Malicious was a taller, thinner woman with long, lean legs and a perfect smile. The three women posed beside their lockers and snapchatted a video.

Shawty Red commentated it. "Last night for my bitch, Champagne. I'm gonna miss yo ass." She stood behind her, humping on her ass, and Malicious humped Shawty Red's ass. After they were finished dancing, Shawty Red looked directly at the camera and said, "I'm gonna miss my bitch," and cried.

They cried. They were all drunk and drinking shots of Cîroc and Snapchatting all night. After the club let out, they hopped into Shawty Red's small BMW and headed to the Waffle House. They smoked and drank and Snapchatted as they listened to Future's new mix tape.

Then, a Chevy Impala and a Volvo blocked them in. Six men jumped out of the cars holding guns. They ordered Shawty Red into the Volvo and shoved Malicious into the Impala. (Where is Champagne?)

After ten minutes of driving, they arrived at an abandoned warehouse area. Two of the men tied rope around their legs and hands, and then TeTe appeared and said, "Give me all of the goddamned phones."

Caleb collected the phones. TeTe shot each of them in the head and said to Caleb, "Snapchat these bitches bleeding. Ho's wanna snapchat everything. Snapchat that.

Then she turned to Caleb and said, "This bitch had every chance in the world to tell me where them niggas was but then she lied."

Chapter 52

The first thing Fresh noticed was her perfume. Bond number 9 Nobu. The next thing he noticed was her dress, a red bandage dress that gripped her ass like a hand. It was backless. He wanted to fuck her on site. Jada invited him in and he stood there speechless. She looked incredible.

"Fresh, I have somewhere I need to be."

"You going out with him?"

"Him who?"

He gave her a side eye and said, "Jada, come on. There is no need to play games. I know you're going out with that nigga."

She sashayed away from him, her heels clacking on the hardwood floor. She felt his eyes on her ass, and she loved that she had that effect on him.

He followed her into the bedroom where she grabbed a gold costume necklace from her jewelry box and said, "Help me fasten this."

He stood behind her trying his best to clasp the tiny-ass necklace. But his huge thumbs were giving him trouble. Mesmerized by the perfume. She was going to meet that nigga. His thigh brushed against her ass.

"Tell me the truth, Jada."

"About what?"

"You're going to see him."

She smiled. "Actually I'm not. Why did you come here?"

"Remember what I asked you about Black?"

"Yes. I spoke with Black."

"And what did he say?"

"He said he didn't do it and I believe him."

"I don't, but that's another story."

She sat on the edge of her bed.

"You ever heard of the Alvarez cartel?"

"On the news and shit."

"The plug is a part of that family, and they now think that I killed the plug."

"So they are after you? Or are going to be after you?"

"Yes."

Jada stood and said, "Okay, and this is the first place you show up? Why in the fuck did you come here? Motherfucker, I ain't even got time to be dodging El Chapo and 'em 'cause you know that motherfucker be escaping prison and shit."

He laughed and said, "It's not like that. You don't have to worry about El Chapo. That's another family. Jada, everything is okay for now."

"How do you know that?"

"They talk to Q on a regular basis. Everything is okay for now."

"I don't want to be involved in this bullshit."

"Jada, Q wants to kill Black."

"Why?"

"I know that Black took that dope. I can't murder him."

"Black didn't do it."

"I'm not here to argue with you."

"I get that; I'm just telling you what I believe."

"And I'm telling you what I believe." He laughed then said, "The motherfucker is convincing. He almost convinced me."

"You spoke to him?"

"He came over my house a few days ago. Saying he didn't have shit to do with it. Then he pulled a gun out on me in my house."

"Why didn't he use that gun?" Jada said. "That proves to me that I'm right. If Black took his shit and he thought you knew about it, he would have killed you. Black is a killer, he don't play."

"I think he did it."

"So what are you going to do?"

"I told Q I wasn't going to kill a brother for the sake of satisfying these wetbacks." They stared at each other for a while.

She said, "What are you going to do?"

"I don't know, but this is what I want you to do: I want you to call Black and let him know that they are after him."

"Who?"

"I don't know."

"You don't think Q would try to kill you, do you?"

"I don't think so."

● ● ●

Black stared incredulously when he opened the door and saw TeTe on his doorstep. She almost never showed up at his place unannounced. She kissed him and held him for a long time as her head rested on his chest. She heard his heartbeat and she was glad she was with him. He invited her in and said, "I thought something was wrong."

"Nothing is wrong. I'm just glad that I have you. I'm happy I have a man like you. I know I don't show that I'm appreciative of you, but I love you, Black."

"Where is all of this coming from?"

"We've been through a lot together. That's all."

He smiled. "I'm actually glad you came over. I have some good news."

"What?"

"I know where two of the Detroit boys live."

"Why haven't you told me this before?"

"Haven't seen you, and that's not something I want to talk about over the phone."

"How did you find them?"

"Champagne found them. She's friends with the Roxy chic I was telling you about, and she went out to their house with them and another friend. She gave me the address."

"Oh really?" TeTe shook her head.

"I knew that if she knew something she would tell me."

"I see," TeTe said, thinking that the bitch should have said something before being killed.

"You should apologize to her."

"Get her on the phone, I will apologize." TeTe knew damn well that there was no way possible for Black to reach a dead woman.

Black dialed her number but it went straight to voicemail. He dialed it again. Voicemail.

"Baby, can we do this some other time?" he asked.

"Yeah."

"There is something I want to tell you."

She raised her eyebrows. She was anticipating bad news.

"What?"

"Remember the FBI agent that I told you about?"

"The one I told you not to fuck with?" Her nostrils flared as she thought of her man even entertaining a damn police officer.

"Yes, him."

"Because of him I'll never have to hustle a day in my life again."

"What are you talking about?"

"He brought me a thousand kilos of coke a few weeks ago, and when I'm done moving them I'll have close to ten million dollars."

"I don't trust him. I don't trust police. It's just me. That's how I am. They'll turn on you."

"Yeah. You're right. But don't worry; it's almost over now."

She eased into his arms and he kissed her. When he released her he said, "After this, I'm done. I mean I have to take care of this issue concerning the motherfuckers that killed my children and your sister, and then I can quit."

"You're never going to quit. Drug dealers don't quit, Black, you know that."

"I'll have close to fourteen million dollars in cash."

"But what's going to stop you from wanting twenty-eight million?"

"I don't need it."

"You don't need fourteen. You want it."

Black turned away from her and said, "Daniels put me in a fucked-up position."

"Who is Daniels?"

"The Fed agent."

"Well of course he put you in fucked-up position, that's what they do."

"Yeah."

"Tell me."

"One of my friends wanted to rob a plug. Well, he wanted me to rob the plug and I refused, didn't want to get involved in that kind of shit right now. But, coincidentally, Daniels robbed and murdered the plug and now my friend thinks I did it."

"That's bad. He don't believe you, huh?"

"Would you?"

"Hell no."

"So that's why I'm certain I'm done with this motherfucker after this is all over."

"So you're going to take fourteen million dollars. How much is the Fed taking?"

"Fourteen."

"It's not over, Black, trust me. He's going to get greedy."

"He can't make me keep moving work for him."

"He's going to threaten to have you locked back up. Threaten you with that old case. He's not going away."

Black said, "I don't want to talk about him no more." He picked up his iPhone and called Champagne. No answer.

Chapter 53

Jabril was asleep on the couch, remote still in hand, when he heard the door get kicked in. He hopped up from the couch and tried to run when a tall, bald black police officer tackled him. He pinned Jabril's hands behind his back and said, "Who else is here?"

"Nobody. I'm gonna tell you right now, if you looking for Molly, ain't shit in here. Not a crumb, so you wasting your motherfucking time."

A light-skinned officer with locks placed a gun to his temple and said, "Motherfucker, speak when you are spoken to. Understand me?"

Jabril trembled.

"Where is your brother?"

"I don't know."

"Call him."

"I'm not calling my brother and telling him to come home to this. I don't get down like that."

Light-Skinned ordered Baldy to stand him up.

One of the officers disappeared into the back room and returned with two scales, twenty thousand dollars in cash, and three guns.

Light-Skinned smiled at Jabril and said, "You're fucked."

Jabril squirmed on the floor. "Listen, man, that's all that's in here. There ain't no dope in here. No Molly. No Weed. No Coke. Just money and these guns that's registered."

"Take his ass out to the car."

Jabril said, "Wait a minute. Where the fuck is the search warrant?"

Light-Skinned knocked the shit out of him with a stick. Jabril was unconscious, blindfolded, and loaded into a small van. They headed to a remote location.

• • •

Jabril came to and seemed to snarl at the smell of burning flesh. He hollered when he realized that it was his own ear burning.

They removed the blindfolds. He saw the woman standing before him. He recognized her immediately. He'd seen pics of her, thought she was dead but she wasn't. She was standing right in front of him. She was a beautiful woman. More beautiful than her pics revealed.

"Good to finally meet you, Jabril."

He couldn't talk. She had him gagged.

He nodded and she leaned forward and said, "Kind of hard to talk when you got something in your mouth."

He kept mumbling with his mouth stuffed.

"Yeah, I have that problem myself when I'm giving head." She leaned forward until their noses touched. "Motherfucker, you killed my sister, and for that you're going to have to pay. Understand me?"

One of her henchmen said, "Do you want me to take the gag out?"

TeTe said, "Did I ask you to take the gag out?"

Jabril mumbled and it sounded like he said he was sorry.

"Too late for all that. We are going to make this short and sweet. Not too much surfing."

She turned to a big stupid-looking nigga with buckteeth named Bull and said, "Pluck his eyeballs out."

"No!" He squirmed and squirmed as two men held him

down while Big Stupid gouged his eyeballs out. They plopped down on the floor.

She made him hold his hands out then she placed the eyeballs in his palms, making him feel squeamish. Who would want to hold their own eyeballs? Blood was oozing from the sockets, and seconds later, she shot him in the head.

• • •

Starr arrived at T.J.'s grandmother's house to pick him up. She would usually just call from her car when she arrived, letting them know that she was there. But today the grandmother invited her in. Starr hesitated. She felt funny going into her house. Her daughter had murdered the love of her life. But she had to forgive her because Trey's mother had forgiven her, and she was T.J.'s grandmother. She turned off the ignition then went inside the house. Mrs. Robinson didn't look like she was aging well at all, but a lot of white people didn't age well.

Mrs. Robinson smiled pleasantly and said, "T.J. is looking for some of his Legos. So I'm assuming it's going to take a few minutes." She looked at Starr's stomach and said, "Congrats."

"Thanks. Am I showing?"

"No, not really." She smiled and said, "T.J. told me."

"He's more excited than I am." Starr said, "T.J., come on."

T.J. appeared with chocolate icing on his little round face. Starr said, "Clean your face."

His grandmother handed him a towel and he wiped his face. She smiled and said, "He loves my cake."

"Yes, he told me about it."

"Mom, just give me a few more minutes. I have to find two more pieces."

"Okay, but I have to go. We're going to your other grandmother's house."

T.J. disappeared into the room.

Mrs. Robinson began asking about other people, making general conversation.

"She's fine. Vacationing right now."

"That's right, T.J. has three grandmothers now."

"Yes. He does."

"So, do you miss him?"

"Trey? Of Course I miss him."

"I know I've said this in the past, but I am so sorry about what happened. There is not a day that goes by that I don't think about what happened."

Starr said, "I don't blame you. Honestly, I don't blame her either. I forgive her."

"I'm glad." She forced a smile. "You know my daughter was really, really sick."

"I knew she had some mental issues."

"Yeah." She sighed and said, "My daughter was influenced."

"You mean somebody that helped her steal the money?"

"No, I mean somebody that helped her kill Trey."

"That's crazy. I don't believe that for one minute. Your daughter acted alone. I'm sure of that."

"I had her cell phone afterward, and I don't know why the police didn't think to look at it, but there had been text exchanges from my daughter and a man in Texas."

Starr's heart raced.

"What did the text say?"

"It was basically urging her to kill him. Telling her she should do it because Trey didn't care about her and that he would never be with her and he never loved her."

"It was a text exchange that went on for about a month"

"What was the man's name."

"Never had a name; it just simply said Plug."

"You have the number?"

"Yes, but the number has been disconnected."

"Can I have that number?"

"I'll give it to you. Do you think he had any enemies down in Houston?"

"I don't know."

"I know Trey was in the drug business."

"We both know that."

"But the thought of this man, whoever he is, manipulating my daughter into killing Trey is hard for me to handle."

Starr studied her face and thought that Q wanted Trey dead. But there had to be another reason for why he would want that. That bullshit about him wanting to be with her was straight up lies.

"I think that she decided to kill Trey, but realized what she had done and killed herself. That's my theory, or perhaps she had been contemplating taking her life. She'd tried to kill herself before."

"T.J.!" Starr yelled out."

"Mom, I can't find it."

Starr asked, "Can he spend the night with you tonight? I really have something that I'm late for."

"Sure."

"T.J., honey, come and give Mommy a kiss."

T.J. ran into Starr's arms and said, "I found it."

She planted a kiss on his cheek and said, "I want you to spend another night with Grandma. Is this okay?"

"Yeah, I like being here."

She planted another kiss on his cheek. "I'll pick you up in the morning. Stay here and protect Grandma. Okay?"

Mrs. Robinson said, "Do you want the number?"

"Yes."

She left and returned with the cell phone.

Starr looked at her oddly. "Why ain't this phone in police custody?"

"They just subpoenaed a copy of the text messages."

"Please text me the number." Starr stormed out of the house and jumped into her car. She peeled out of the driveway, replaying what she had just heard. She called Jada, who picked up on the first ring.

"Hello."

"I'm so upset right now," Starr said.

"What's wrong, baby?"

"You will never guess what I heard?"

"Starr, what's wrong? Where are you?"

"I'm headed home."

"What's wrong? Please tell me what's wrong."

"I think Q encouraged that crazy-ass white chick to kill Trey."

"What?"

"Yes. Q! He's not the man that I thought he was."

"How did you find this out? How do you know it's true?"

"I spoke with Jessica's mother today, and she said there were text messages in the phone from Q to Jessica. He knew she was crazy and he took advantage of her."

"What?"

"Yeah."

"Oh damn. This is too much for me to handle. I'm going to call Shantelle to see if she know anything about it."

"I don't ever want to see this motherfucker again in my life."

Jada could hear the breathing on the phone. "You need to calm down, baby girl."

"Yeah, you're right," Starr said. Then she heard someone honking their horn. When she glanced up at the traffic light, she realized she was riding straight through a red light. Starr slammed on brakes.

Jada heard the brakes screeching. She heard Starr scream. She heard the collision. "Starr, you okay? You okay?"

Jada's mind went back to the day that Lani died. God, she hoped that this wasn't the end for her best friend. She didn't know if she could take listening to another friend die. "Starr!" she screamed.

"I'm here. I'm okay."

"Thank God you're okay. Where are you?"

"I'm at the corner of Courtland and Currier Street."

"I'm on my way."

Starr's eyes were burning because of the airbag. She struggled to unbuckle the seatbelt when she noticed that there was a puddle of blood between her legs.

"Starr? I'm on my way."

Starr struggled to open the door because it was mangled and stuck.

A Middle-Eastern man kicked out the window, open the passenger door, and helped Starr out of the vehicle. The man said, "You're bleeding really bad. We have to get you to the hospital."

Starr said, "I'm pregnant and I've just lost my baby!"

Chapter 54

Craig Matthew still hadn't gotten adjusted to jail life. He did not like someone telling him when to go to bed, when to wake up and when he could use the phone. He couldn't go to the store. And the worst part of it all, he had to be associating with all the low-life losers that he would never ever be affiliated with in the real world.

His sentencing was still months away. So he had to get adjusted to this very bad situation. Today was commissary day, and he wanted to have himself a little jailhouse feast that consisted of oodles of noodles soup and crackers. Slim Jim sausages, and cheese nachos.

His cellmate, a white child molester named Bob Latimer, went out into the day room because he couldn't stand the smell of the nachos.

All I need now is a glass of wine, he told himself. Then he noticed Fy-Head. Sculpted. He cracked the door of his cell and invited her in.

She was hesitant at first but finally entered the cell.

"Sit on my bed."

She sat down.

He offered her some nachos and soups. She declined the

soups. He said, "Do I smell perfume?"

She smiled.

"How in the hell did you get perfume in here?"

"A woman never tells all of her secrets, didn't you know that?"

"Would you like a soda? I have Sprite."

She stood and peered outside to see where the station officer was. He was reading a magazine. Inmates weren't supposed to be in other inmates' cells.

She sat back on the bed.

He ate a handful of nachos and said, "I can't believe we're friends."

"I know."

"When do you go to court?"

"I don't know, in a couple of weeks. I'm hoping I get out of here."

"Honestly, I didn't mean for her to die."

"Your wife?"

"No, your friend."

"Hey, what's done is done. I'd prefer we not talk about her," Fy-Head said.

She forced a smile and said, "So who are you hiding from?"

"There is an MC that wants my ass."

"MC?"

"Motorcycle Club. Gang really."

"For what?"

"The guy that killed your friend was a part."

"So you ratted on them?"

"I saved my ass."

"Whatever."

"I have to be going." She stood up and so did he, his eyes looking down at her tight jumpsuit.

She turned and smiled. "Don't be looking at my ass, white boy. You know this is off limits to you and everybody else."

"Why does it have to be like this?"

"Are you crazy? I know you know my status—"

He cut her off. And stuck his tongue down her throat.

· · ·

Black met up with Daniels at their usual location to give him the rest of the money. Daniels loaded the money in the back of his pickup and said, "I'm surprised that you came."

"Why? You thought I wasn't going to pay you?"

"You were pretty pissed off the last time I saw you."

"I'm over it now. It is what it is."

"Does that mean we can work again?"

"I got business to take care of."

"Oh yeah, right. Gotta get back at those petty-ass Detroit drug dealers."

"Gotta do it for my kids. You got kids?"

"I do. I told you that already."

"Well then, you understand."

"I can get them for you."

"I don't want to be in bed with you for the rest of my life. You got your money, now will you leave me the fuck alone?"

"In two weeks, Q is going to get a shipment and I'm going to take it."

"Q?"

"You know, Q? Fresh's friend."

"I don't know what you're talking about."

"Black, I know by now that they think you set the connect up to get robbed. Right now there's probably a hit on your head."

"You motherfucker you."

"Black, let's make this money."

"I don't want to fuck with you. At all."

"I kill the Detroit boys and then take out Fresh and Q. Clean hits. Nobody has to know. Nobody knows about the plug, do they?"

"I don't want to work with you, bruh."

"Don't let this come back to bite you in the ass, man."

Chapter 55

When Starr woke up from surgery, she saw Jada. She smiled and Jada held her hands. She spotted her mother and father and sister, Meeka. "The baby is gone, I guess."

"Yes." Jada nodded. "But it's okay, you're still young. You'll get pregnant again and you'll have another one. We'll have one together."

Starr began to sob.

Ace, Starr's father, said, "Can someone please tell me what happened?"

"She ran a red light and was hit by a Hummer."

"I don't know why those damn things are still on the road. Thank God you're okay, baby!"

"I'm not okay. I lost my baby! I want my baby!"

Jada said, "Calm down, Starr."

"I don't want to be calm."

Q and Fresh entered the recovery room.

Q rushed to Starr's side and said, "What's wrong?"

Starr screamed at him and said, "Get the hell away from me! It's your fault!"

Q looked confused.

Ace looked at Q and said, "Hormones, you know how

women can be."

"Hormones, my ass. I want him the fuck out of my room."

Starr's mother, Wanda, knew something was wrong. Starr rarely cursed in front of her parents.

Ace said, "Leave."

Fresh grabbed Q by the arm and led him out of the hospital room.

When he was gone, Ace said, "What's wrong with you? Why did you want him out of here?"

"I don't want to see him."

"Why not?"

"He is not the man I thought he was."

Meeka said, "Slick ass probably got somebody else pregnant."

Starr buzzed for the nurse and when she appeared she asked, "How long do I have to stay in this hospital?"

●   ●   ●

A big collection box on the counter of the club had three women's faces plastered on it. Black asked the girl behind the counter. "What is this collection for?"

"To help the family of the girls."

"What happened?"

"They were murdered."

"All three of them?"

"Yeah, the same night. I'm surprised you ain't hear about it. Some sick person murdered them on Snapchat. It's been all over the news and social media."

Black looked closely at the picture of Champagne.

"Yeah, hers is especially sad; she was moving back to St. Louis."

Black removed a thousand dollars from his pocket and placed it in the collection jar. He darted to the parking lot and drove straight to TeTe's house.

TeTe had a towel on her head when she opened the door. She was ready for bed.

"I didn't know you were coming."

Black barged right in without being invited.

"What's wrong, babe?"

"You killed her."

It seemed to have gone right over her head because she didn't even respond to it. Instead, she said, "I caught up with those Detroit boys."

"What?"

"I used the address that you had given me and it was dead on the money."

"So they are gone?"

"One of them is. We're going to find the other one."

"We? You killed Champagne."

"She's dead?" TeTe tried to sound surprised.

"Come one, TeTe. You know she's dead."

TeTe dried her hair with the towel then removed it. "How am I supposed to know who killed the bitch. I got my own hoes to keep up with."

"Okay, you didn't do it?"

"No." She turned away from him. "No, I didn't do it." She looked him in the eyes and said, "I thought you said that you had just seen her."

"I did. She was murdered a day after I last saw her."

"And you think it was me?"

Black threw his hands up.

She made her way up to him, stroked his chest, and said, "I'm sorry. I didn't know that she had given you the address. I didn't know she had helped us. I saw her on Snapchat partying with these dudes and shit, and I thought she was lying. Honestly, I didn't know. I'm sorry."

"You murdered my friend. This is a life you took. It's not like some accident. You just can't say I'm sorry and everything goes back to normal."

"Black, my twin sister was murdered. And your children were killed. You think I give a fuck about some stripper bitch?"

He sighed. She was right, and he had not considered how the loss of her sister may have affected her.

"And if you remember, Black, I'm in this shit because of you. I was living a normal life until I started seeing your ass. They shot your car up with me in it."

"I didn't want you to retaliate."

"Nobody shoots at me and gets away with it, and nobody kills one of my own and gets away with it." She paced, suds from the shampoo dripping onto her shoulders.

"I'm sorry for getting you involved."

I'm sorry for killing your little bitch."

"What are you talking about?"

"Black, you think I didn't know that you've fucked her? I could see how she looked at you."

Black said, "You're out of control right now, and I can't have that."

"What are you going to do, Black?" She laughed, grabbed the towel, and dried herself off.

"I'm leaving."

"Don't you fucking leave, Black. Don't leave out that door; you're going to regret it."

"I don't think you and I can co-exist. You're too much like a nigga."

"Fuck you, Black!"

He walked toward the door and she chased him. When she reached him, she jumped on his back and beat the fuck out of him.

He flailed his body around trying to get rid of her, but she held on tight, clawing and scratching. "Don't you fucking leave me. You will regret this, motherfucker. I gave you my all and this is how you treat me?"

He finally flung her to the floor. She sat there on the floor crying, the wells of her eyes filled.

Chapter 56

A week after Starr was released from the hospital, she was back at work and was in the front of the studio when Terrell walked in. She dug into her pocket and handed Brooke thirty dollars. "Will you go to Chipotle and get me a bowl with brown rice, steak, mild sauce, sour cream, and corn? And get yourself whatever you want."

Brooke smiled and said, "Thanks so much."

Terrell approached Starr and said, "Miscarried the baby?"

"That's what I told you over the phone."

"You told that to my Voice mail."

"I told you."

"What happened?"

"I was in a car wreck. Did you even listen to the voice mail?"

"I did. Why do you think I'm here?"

"I don't know why you are here; I told you what happened." Starr saw pain in his eyes. She tried very hard not to make eye contact.

"I'm here because I called your phone and you didn't answer."

"I didn't answer because I didn't have nothing else to say. I'm mean, what is there to say? I lost the baby."

"I want to know what happened."

"What part of I was in a car wreck don't you understand?"

"How?"

"I was on the phone, and I was upset about something and wasn't paying attention to what I was doing. I ran the light and was hit."

"And you're okay?"

"Yes. Thanks for asking."

"You're okay, but my baby died."

"It was my baby, too."

He laughed and said, "You are walking around very comfortable."

"What are you saying, sir?"

"I'm saying it ain't fair that you are living and my baby is dead."

Starr stared him. Did this silly motherfucker just say that he wished she was dead? "I'm sorry this happened. I didn't mean for this to happen, and I know how you must feel. I feel the same way."

"You don't feel the same way that I feel. You wanted to kill the baby in the first place. Then you had your little dope boyfriend show up at my place to threaten me. Please. Get the fuck out of here with that."

"No, you get out of here. Get out of here right now before I call the police on you. Since that's the only thing your bitch ass understand is running down to the police station taking out warrants like a little bitch."

"Baby killer!"

Brooke eased up behind him and tossed both bowls of Chipotle on his head.

He turned and charged toward Brooke, but Starr wedged herself between them and said, "You get out of here right now or I'm calling the police on yo ass."

Sour cream, corn, and hot sauce were resting on the top of his head. He turned and rushed for the door. Before he left he yelled, "Baby killer!"

Starr plummeted to the floor and sobbed. Brooke sat down beside her and tried to console her.

• • •

Black's electric blue flannel shirt looked nice against his skin. It was the first thing she noticed. The second thing she noticed was that he looked sad. She invited him in and poured him a shot of Cîroc. "What's wrong?"

"It's TeTe."

"What's up with her?"

"She's out of control."

"You knew that from the start."

He took a shot and downed it. "What's up with Mari?"

"His attorney filed a motion to get him out."

"Out?"

"Yeah, seems like the cops coerced the statement and he may get out for a retrial."

Black smiled. "So what's been up? Why did you invite me here?"

"Well, you know that Fresh n'em think that you robbed the connect?"

"Please, Jada." Black stood and was headed toward the door. "I don't want to hear this shit. You can believe what you want to believe. I got enough shit to worry about."

Jada cut him off and blocked his path. She looked him in the eyes and said, "I don't believe you did it."

"So why in the fuck are you telling me this?"

"Because Q wants you dead."

"What?"

"The cartel believe that Fresh had Diego killed."

"He wanted me to kill the man, and as far as I know he could have killed him," Black lied, knowing damn well who had killed Diego.

"He didn't do it."

"How do you know?"

"I'm fucking the man."

"That don't mean shit. I don't know half the shit that TeTe is into."

"But she is a lunatic."

"Okay, Fresh and Q want me dead."

"I didn't say Fresh."

"Q wants me dead."

"Yes. He does, so I want you to be careful, Black. I don't know what I would do if you were murdered. I don't want to even think about that."

"Good, because it's not going to happen."

"I know."

"So is there anything else you need to tell me?"

"No."

"You do believe me, don't you, Jada? You're not just saying that?"

"I believe you. I just want you to get out of town."

Black laughed and said, "Nobody is running me out of Atlanta. I was born and raised here."

"That's how I feel."

"I just feel sorry for Starr. She's with a dude like that? She may have upgraded in money but she downgraded because he's a clown."

"They're not together."

"What?"

"She found out that Q had something to do with Trey's death."

"Yeah?"

"It's a long story."

"I don't have time for a long story. I gotta go."

She said, "Before you go, can I get a hug?" Black embraced her and his hands traveled down her waist until he was gripping her ass. She didn't resist or push him back. He held it for a while, and before they knew it, they were kissing.

She said, "We need to stop."

"Yeah."

"Be careful."

"I'm good."

Jada said, "What just happened, keep that between me and you."

"Of course."

"It was a mistake."

"For sho!"

She approached him and they kissed again. His hand slid down to her ass. He removed her jeans and yanked her panties down. Jada was standing there in just her bra.

He kissed her and wrestled her bra strap off.

Jada's mind was on Lani. She was betraying Lani and Shamari at the same time, but right now, she couldn't explain why she wanted to be fucked by Black. All she knew was that she wanted him inside her.

Black had slid out of his underwear; his dick was standing at attention. Big. Thick. Slightly curved. He pushed her back on her sofa. She was on her back with her legs open. He dove between her legs and kissed her thighs, her vulva, and finally her clitoris. She ran her fingers through his locks and pushed his head farther down.

"Oh God, Black, you feel so good."

He continued to lick her clit, kissing it, sucking it, toying with it. His tongue traveled up to her navel, circling her belly button, and he sucked her tits. He kissed each nipple slowly.

"You make me feel so damn good."

"Turn over." When she turned over on her stomach, he saw those massive ass checks and his dick got harder. For a second he was guilty. Remembering how Shamari had accused him of fucking her, though he hadn't been. How he said he would never do something like that, but now he was doing exactly what he said he would never do, and she was doing what she said that she would never do. He hated that he was so weak, but damn that ass was looking so amazing to him.

He entered her from behind and she said, "Push further," and he pushed as far as he could.

He smacked her ass and she yelled, "Yes, daddy. Yes, daddy, punish me." Black kept pounding. Yanking her hair. Spanking her.

He stood her up and walked with her. He fucked her standing up and then finally ended on his back as she rode him in the reverse cowboy position until he came inside her. His member remained hard and he kept stroking until he exploded inside her once more.

She stood and walked to the shower, his eyes trailing her ass. She didn't say a word. She showered and when she came back, he was sitting on the sofa butt naked.

She tossed him a washcloth and a towel and said, "I feel guilty about what we just did."

"Me too."

"Why did we do it?"

"I don't know about you, but I wanted to do this for a long time."

"Yes. I suppose I did too. But how can I call myself Lani's friend, doing some shit like this?"

"Lani is gone. Shamari is gone. I love both of them but shit happens."

"I suppose, but Mari is on his way home."

"And we still love him. We're human, Jada. You're a good person. I'm a good person. There is a lot of people that say we're both fucked up. We're flawed but we take care of those that take care of us."

"I feel a little better, but I can't help but think about Lani."

Black headed to the shower. When he returned ten minutes later she said, "Thanks, Black, for all you have done. Nobody is to ever know about this." And when she opened the door to let him out, Tank stood in the doorway.

Black said, "Can I help you?"

When Jada saw Tank, she said, "Come in."

Tank said, "Who the fuck is this nigga?"

"Who the fuck are you, clown?"

Black reached for his gun on his waist and Jada said, "No, Black." Then she said to Tank. "This is my homeboy, Black. He's a friend of my ex's. He was just leaving."

Tank and Black were still staring at each other.

"Jada is like a sister to me, partner," Black said.

Tank said, "You know what, Jada? This is just too much drama fucking with you."

"Do what you gotta do, nigga. Don't nobody got time for yo married ass anyhow."

Tank turned to walk away and said to Black, "You can have that bitch."

Black turned to Jada and said, "I'm sorry."

"It's okay."

"Talk to you later."

"Bye."

Chapter 57

Fresh and Q were out on Q's terrace eating egg whites and turkey sausage. Q said, "We're going to need to get rid of Black."

"Why?"

"You know why. Diego's uncle thinks that you robbed and killed his nephew."

Fresh said, "I don't understand you, man. A few weeks ago, you telling me not to fuck with this dude, and now you're concerned about what might happen?"

"And you dealt with him for what reason?"

Q had no response.

"I'll tell you why you dealt with him. It was because you're greedy as fuck."

"But we were going to kill him because of what he did to Rico. At least that's what you said." Fresh had a smirk on his face.

"I wanted to kill him on my time."

"You know what, Q? I don't think you were going to do shit. Something is not adding up."

"A few days before Diego was murdered, I met up with him and told him not to do business with you. Told him I wanted to do business with him. His cousin Gordo was going to kill him."

"His cousin was going to kill for us? For Rico?"

"Yes and no."

"What do you mean?"

"Gordo wants to supply Atlanta, and Diego was in the way. But the fact that we wanted him dead made it an easy thing to do because he wants to do business with me. He needs me."

Fresh shook his head. Damn, Q was one calculating motherfucker.

"Q, what was the real reason you wanted Trey dead?"

"I told you."

"I don't believe you. Trey gets killed, you move to Atlanta and try to hit on his girl. What the fuck is up? Was Trey in your way?"

"Maybe."

"You wanted him dead because he could control Atlanta."

"My connect wanted to meet Trey."

"And you were afraid that he would help Trey lock down all of Atlanta, wasn't you?"

"If Trey took over Atlanta, they wouldn't need me."

"What about your other distributors?"

"Atlanta is the major hub."

Fresh sighed and said, "Damn, I don't know you at all, bruh."

"So all that talk about you getting out of the game was just bullshit?"

"I knew that if I told them that, they would beg me; they would need me. They would lower prices and do whatever they had to do to keep me in the fold."

"You let one of your best friends get killed. Just to prove a point?"

"Fresh, we need to kill Black."

"Because he killed someone that you and I both wanted to kill? What kind of sense does that make?"

"It doesn't matter. This sends a message to the Alvarez cartel that we are on their side."

"And why do we want to be on their side?"

"We can take over Atlanta. Hundreds of thousands of

bricks of coke."

"Dude, I ain't down with this shit." Fresh stood and said, "Fuck you, dude. You got too many goddamn secrets."

• • •

Starr was surprised when her father, Ace, showed up at her condo. He almost never came by. She'd been there for almost a year and he'd come two times. She invited him in and he marveled at the expensive furniture and décor. "So this is how the cheese and wine crowd live."

"Daddy, you've been here before, and you know I ain't in no damn cheese and wine crowd."

Ace's thumbs were cuffing his belt loops as he stared at his daughter.

"So what brings you here?"

"I was a little worried about you. The other day when you was in the hospital and you were screaming at Q to get out. What was that about?"

"Nothing to worry about, daddy."

Ace sat on the edge of the sofa. "I don't believe you."

She looked away from him. She hated lying to him.

"What did Q do to you?"

Silence.

"Did he make you lose my grandbaby? Did he put his hands on you? Because if I find out that he did, ain't nothing going to stop me from killing him or him killing me. You know I ain't lying, don't you?"

"I know."

"Look at me."

They made eye contact before she turned away. "Tell me what's going on."

"It's Trey." She started crying.

"What about Trey? And why are you crying?"

"Q is not the person that I thought he was."

"What?" He rushed to her side and said, "Tell me, baby, what is wrong and what about Trey?"

"Q killed Trey."

Ace laughed and said, "Baby you know that Q didn't kill

Trey. That crazy white bitch killed Trey, not Q."

"No. I found out that Q manipulated her and she killed Trey."

"Bullshit."

"Daddy, I saw the text messages. The messages were from Q urging her to kill him."

"This is crazy."

"She was crazy. She tried to kill herself before. She suffered from bipolar disorder and she tried to kill herself. So I think when she killed Trey, she realized what she had done and decided to take her own life, or she planned it from the start."

"This is ridiculous."

"Daddy, I didn't want to believe it, but I saw the text."

"So when did you learn this?"

"Right before the wreck."

"So you were upset?"

"Yes."

He approached her and they hugged. He said, "Don't worry, baby. I got you."

Chapter 58

Fresh had flown to Houston to meet up with a longtime friend. He wanted to buy some work to take back to Atlanta. He had made up his mind that he wasn't going to deal with Q anymore. He called his friend Jabo as soon as he retrieved his bags from baggage claims.

"What's going on? Did you touch down, baby!" Jabo said.

"Yes, I'm here."

"Perfect. Give me a few hours, then we can meet up and chop it up."

"Good, I can go see my mom and then my baby mom and my son."

It was six o'clock when he met Jabo at Wings & Things.

Jabo was a diesel, dark-skinned dude with a block head and red eyes. Fresh and Jabo had been friends since they were kids. Their mothers were friends and they played together as kids. He was a year older than Fresh and like Fresh he had a small son.

Jabo said, "I ain't think I would see you again. I heard you were up in the A, tripling your profit."

"I don't know about all that."

"So tell me, what's going on?"

"I need something, just a few bricks to hold me until I get a connect."

"My homie, Puff, has it for eighteen."

"Eighteen is a little high."

"These are niggas, not Mexicans, so you know it's going to be a little higher, homie."

"Is he cool?" Jabo said.

"You know me, homie! We been playing with each other since diapers."

"Yeah." He smiled. He was comfortable with Jabo. They were like brothers, since each of their mothers had only one son. They used to call themselves brothers when they were kids.

"I'm going back to my mama's spot out in Sugarland. You can meet me there if you want, and I'll give you the money."

"I'll do even better. I'll take you with me. Let you travel with your money."

"You don't have to do all of that."

"I want to."

"Okay, well pick me up at mom's in two hours."

• • •

Three and a half hours later, Jabo pulled up in front of Fresh's mother's house. He was late. His son had been sick and he had to make a dash to the store to pick up some meds. Fresh ran outside carrying a backpack. Jabo was listening to Roosh Williams, a local Houston rapper.

"How much you got in the bag?" Jabo asked.

"Thirty-six racks."

"Looks like more in there than that."

"I brought my gun."

Jabo laughed and said, "Everything is going to go smoothly."

"I believe you."

• • •

Twenty-five minutes later, they arrived at Sunnyside and Fresh said, "Damn, homie, I ain't know we were going to the hood."

Jabo said, "Look at me." The made eye contact and Jabo said, "Who am I to you?"

"My brother."

"It's going to be okay."

And Fresh was totally at ease. He calmed down and they drove up a hill and a long winding road to a house at the end of the street. There was a small park across the street. Kids were on hover boards and bikes and skateboards.

Jabo said, "It's the hood, but it's okay over here."

The sight of the children playing made him relax a little. Jabo was the first to get out of the car and Fresh was behind him.

"You left the gun in the car?" Jabo asked.

"Why would I do that?"

"Take the gun back, homie. I got you. I just don't want nobody thinking I'm trying some slick shit."

Fresh marched back to the car. He didn't think it was a good idea. But whatever. He concealed the gun inside the car. Jabo stood on the porch and waited for Fresh. Fresh ran up on the porch and Jabo tapped on the door.

"Who is it?"

"Jab."

The door opened and a black-ass man with gold teeth, scraggly braids, and burnt lips stood there shirtless, smoking a blunt.

Jabo gave him a pound. "E, this is my homie, Fresh. Well, we're more like brothers."

"You fux with Jab, you fux with me."

Seconds later a slim, lighter complexioned dude name DeSean came out. DeSean was an inch shorter than Fresh and had freckles around his nose. Fresh spotted a gun print by DeSean's waist and wondered why in the fuck didn't he bring his heat.

"Let's go to the kitchen." DeSean led them to the kitchen where there was another man. A bigger guy, unidentified, and he just nodded at Fresh.

Fresh removed the backpack and dumped the money on the table and said, "It's too late to be scared now. If you're going to rob me, go ahead and take this shit right now."

Jabo looked at him like he was crazy.

"This shit don't feel right."

DeSean looked at the big dude and they laughed. "We don't rob around here, homie." He reached in the cabinet and pulled out two bricks.

Fresh relaxed.

"That ain't how we do business. We do good business around here." DeSean passed him a knife and said, "Taste it."

Fresh cut into the package, tasted it with a thumb, and said, "It's good."

"And there is more where that came from. Get more and I will lower the ticket."

"Just like that?"

"Look, Dawg, you cool with Jabs, you cool with us."

Jab grinned and said, "I told you they were cool, my G."

Fresh loaded the coke into the bag and they headed out the door. He said, "I want to get a few more before I head to Atlanta."

"Okay, just let me know and I'll let DeSean know."

Chapter 59

Fy-Head and Craig had talked the jailers into letting them become cellmates while they waited on their court dates. They would eat together, watch TV together, and play cards and chess. Everyone in the protective custody pod considered the two of them a couple, and it appeared as if they were the perfect couple. Craig had urged that when Fy-Head gets released, they should get married. Fy-Head was adamant, saying that she didn't think she could be with a man that was facing a life sentence, and they should just enjoy the moment. And enjoying the moment they were. They sat in the cell and discussed over nachos the meaning of life.

"My biggest accomplishments were my children."

"I beg to differ, Dr. Matthews."

"Huh?"

"Your biggest accomplishment was sculpting this big old juicy ass of mine." Fy-Head stood and twerked.

Craig loved her because she made him laugh and she had a forgiving heart. He wished they would have been this close when they were on the street.

"I have a question."

"No sex."

He made a sad face.

"Am I really that good?"

"The best," Craig claimed.

"I'll see if I can find a glove and maybe, just maybe, I'll let you put it in for a moment."

He smiled. "But that was not my question."

"What is the question?"

"How did you find it in your heart to forgive me?"

"I don't know." She looked away. "I'm just a forgiving person."

"I don't know how I could ever be as forgiving."

"You do know that you can't marry me, right?"

"No? Why? Don't you love me?"

"I love you."

"But you're not in love with me?"

Fy-Head's hands rested on her hips and she said, "I'm about to get out in a few days. I can't marry a man that is going to do the rest of his life behind bars."

"You can't marry a man that is going to do the rest of his life behind bars, or you can't marry a killer?"

"Not my place to judge."

"You're going to forget about me when you get out."

"Let's just enjoy the moment."

"I'm going to make more nachos."

"Good. I'll ask the officer if I can use the iron, and I'll make grill cheese sandwiches."

"You're so resourceful."

He smiled and said, "Before you go out there, can I see it?"

"See what?"

"My biggest accomplishment."

She dropped her pants and he stared at her gigantic ass in awe.

Chapter 60

Shamari had been surprised when his case manager had summoned him into the office and ordered him to pack his things. There was a court order for him to be released. He stood there for a few minutes with his hands on his hips and said, "There must be some kind of mistake. I have life. Are you kidding me?"

The case manager showed him the order. "You're getting out. This is the court order."

He smiled and said, "I can't believe this shit." Shamari headed back to his cell and got possession of the pictures that Jada and his sister had sent him. He left everything else, from food to headphones to sweat suits, for his cellmate.

An hour later, he was walking out of the gates. His sister and her boyfriend Hunch were waiting. He hopped into the Chrysler and they remained parked at the prison. Hunch was eating a box of Popeye's chicken and he passed Shamari a wing.

"I know you want a piece of this, boy."

Shamari grinned as he chomped down on the chicken.

His sister Tangie said, "So what happened? How did you get out?"

"The cop that arrested me was dirty, and the guy that told on me recanted his statement. So I'm out waiting on a new trial."

His sister was still parked in front of the prison and Shamari said, "Will you get the hell away from here? I don't want to see this place."

She laughed and fired up the car.

"Tangie, can you pass me the phone?" She passed the phone and he dialed Black's number. He didn't get an answer so he dialed the number again.

"Hello."

"Black boy!"

"Who this?"

"It's Mari."

"Oh, you got a new cell phone in there?"

"I'm out, bruh. Got an immediate release today."

"You lying."

"No."

"Where you at?"

"I'm heading to my sister's house now. I'll text you the address."

"Are you really out?"

"Yeah, nigga, what you want me to do, take a selfie to prove to you that I'm out?"

"I believe you. I got some running around to do then I'll come by. Does Jada know you're out?"

"No. You're the first person that knows I'm out."

Black suddenly felt guilty about having sex with Jada.

"I just want you to know that I love you, man, and I appreciate everything you done for me while I was in."

"It was nothing, bruh. I know you would have done the same. I'll see you tonight."

• • •

It was 7:16 p.m. when Fresh and Jabo arrived back at DeSean's house. Fresh had another $54,000 to buy three more kilos. Same set as before. DeSean answered the door and ushered Fresh and Jabo into the kitchen where the big stupid-looking dude was waiting. Fresh gave him the money and he gave Fresh the coke. The men shook hands and Fresh said that he would be back in a few weeks to buy more. DeSean said, "I'll give you my number if it's okay with Jabo?"

"Me and Fresh are like brothers. Give me the number."

Fresh said, "I'll bring him with me anyway."

"Listen, man, we're all family."

DeSean exchanged numbers with him. The big stupid dude and DeSean walked them out to the car.

When they got to the top of the hill, Fresh noticed two men following closely behind in a car.

Fresh said to Jabo, "Bruh, that black Maxima is following us."

Jabo looked in the mirror and said, "They ain't thinking about us. You getting all paranoid."

They made a left. The Maxima made a left.

Fresh removed his gun that was sitting under the seat. "I'm telling you, bruh, they following us."

Fresh reclined in the seat and cocked the gun.

The Maxima pulled up beside them and opened fire. A bullet ripped through Jabo's chest and the car fishtailed before slamming into a pole.

Jabo slumped over on the steering wheel, barely breathing.

Fresh opened the door and crawled out of the car, staying low and crawling underneath the car.

The Maxima came to a stop beside them and two men jumped out and fired more shots in the side of the door and into the head of Jabo. Blood was oozing from his head and chest.

Fresh heard one of the shooters say, "Where is the other nigga?"

"Where the fuck is the dope?"

"He was carrying a backpack."

Fresh was lying underneath the car, his heart pounding, about to explode through his chest.

He could see the shoes of the two men. Nike Huaraches and a pair of LeBron's. They were going to kill him.

Fresh sprayed his gun, hitting both men's ankles. Fourteen

bullets discharged from his gun, eight bullets hitting the assailants. The men fell and Fresh had a better aim at the chest and stomach, so he began firing fourteen more shots into the men's bodies.

A small crowd gathered outside near the scene.

One of the men was still moving—the motherfucker he'd seen at the house, the one with the black-ass lips.

Fresh stood over him and fired six more shots into his chest then struck out running.

Chapter 61

The sound of a dripping faucet was all they heard. Fy-Head lay beside Craig in the tiny bed. Her big, manufactured ass pinning him against the concrete wall. Their cells were locked down and the lights in the common area were off. The fat-ass guard on duty was accessing Facebook from his phone. The next head count would be in a couple of hours. His hands on her waist. He had a handful of her ass and said, "I wish you didn't have to go."

She turned toward him and they kissed.

"You're going to miss me?" She smiled.

"You know I am."

"I'll come visit."

His eyes lit up. "Promise me."

"I promise you."

"I should have picked you."

"Picked me to kill?"

"No. You know what I mean."

"Well, you know she was the glamorous one, and you men love glamour."

"My downfall."

"You know I'm going to miss you too."

"Can we make love just one more time?"

"I would prefer that you fuck me. You know, rough sex. Choke me, spank me, spit on me. Make me call you daddy."

He smiled.

She got up and his eyes were on her ass. She looked under her mattress and retrieved a latex glove. She cut one of the fingers with a blade and passed it to him. A makeshift condom.

He was inside her and she said, "Choke me, daddy."

And he choked her as hard as he could.

Still she managed to say, "Choke me harder."

He relented and she became angry.

"What hell are you doing?" she demanded.

"Are you trying to make me kill you?"

"I'm just trying to get off."

He placed his hands around her neck. Feeling her Adam's apple reminded him that she was a he.

"Choke me."

He choked her as hard he could until she tapped his arm. He released her from his grip and lay on top of him. They kissed.

She said, "I'm really going to miss you, daddy." Before he could respond, she slit his throat with a razor. The blood spurted from his neck. His prints on her throat. He'd choked her. He had killed before and her story would be he tried to kill her. She pressed the distress button and got the attention of the fat-ass officer.

• • •

It was 10:46 p.m. and Black was parked where he and Daniels usually met.

Daniels drove up. A white man with a huge neck sat on the passenger side. They both hopped out.

Black lowered his radio and said, "Who's your company?"

"Agent Malarkey." Daniels turned to Malarkey. Malarkey was a six-year field officer and he had been working on the West Coast up until a few years ago when he was transferred to the Atlanta Division.

Black laughed and said, "I guess now is the part where you lock me up."

Daniels and Malarkey looked at each other and laughed.

Black passed him the last of the money he had owed him. "Go ahead and count it."

Daniels said, "No need to count it; I trust you. You know I trust you." Malarkey tossed the money in the back of the cab.

"So you're really done?"

"I'm done, bro."

"Your boy is out. I helped get your boy out."

"It's not about my boy."

Malarkey said, "Give me a reason why I shouldn't call my friends at Homeland Security and tell them to indict yo ass."

"Do what you want."

"Or, I can lock that crazy bitch of yours up. You know the one that pimps the whores?"

"Look, bruh, I'm done."

Malarkey removed his gun and pointed it at Black. "What's going to stop me from blowing your goddamn head off?"

Black looked at Daniels with pleading eyes. He didn't want to die out here in the middle of nowhere. "So you're going to let this shit go down?"

"Black, we made you into a rich man. You've made more money than you have ever made in your life with us."

"So I owe you?"

"You owe us."

"So what do you want from me?"

"I have a shipment of two thousand kilos of heroin. I need you to help me get rid of it."

"I can't."

Malarkey fired a shot into Black's leg.

"You have a chance right now, Black. You going to help us or not?"

Black hesitated.

Daniels removed his gun and fired a single shot that ripped through Malarkey's head.

"What the fuck! You killed your own partner?"

Daniels stood over Malarkey's body then bent forward to take his pulse. He knew the man was dead. He turned to Black said, "Hold this for a second."

Black took possession of the gun.

"No, you killed him," Daniels said.

"Oh, hell no, you ain't pinning this shit on me."

Daniels removed Malarkey's gun from his body and fired two shots into Black's chest cavity.

Black stumbled back and said, "You...motherfucker," and took his last breath.

Daniels removed his radio and said, "Officer down! Officer down!"

The end.

GET A FREE eBOOK!

Enjoyed this book?
If you enjoyed this book please write a review and email it to me at kevinelliott3@gmail.com, and get a FREE ebook.

K. Elliott Book Order Form
PO Box 12714
Charlotte NC 28220

Book Name	Quantity	Price	Shipping/ Handling	Total
Dear Summer		X $14.95	+ $3.00 per book	
Dilemma		X $14.95	+ $3.00 per book	
Entangled		X $13.95	+ $3.00 per book	
Godsend Series 1–5		X $14.95	+ $3.00 per book	
Godsend Series 6–10		X $14.95	+ $3.00 per book	
Kingpin Wifeys Vol. 1		X $14.95	+ $3.00 per book	
Kingpin Wifeys Vol. 2		X $14.95	+ $3.00 per book	
Kingpin Wifeys Vol. 3		X $14.95	+ $3.00 per book	
Kingpin Wifeys Vol. 4		X $14.95	+ $3.00 per book	
Kingpin Wifeys Vol. 5		X $14.95	+ $3.00 per book	
Kingpin Wifeys Vol. 6		X $14.95	+ $3.00 per book	
Street Fame		X $14.95	+ $3.00 per book	
Treasure Hunter		X $15.00	+ $3.00 per book	
			TOTAL	

Mailing Address

Name:

Mailing Address:

City	State	Zip

Method Of Payment
[   ] Check [   ] Money Order

Thank you for your support

About the Author

K. Elliott, aka The Well Fed Black Writer, penned his first novel, Entangled, in 2003. Although he was offered multiple signing deals, Elliott decided to found his own publishing company, Urban Lifestyle Press.

Bookstore by bookstore, street vendor by street vendor, Elliott took to the road selling his story. He did not go unnoticed, selling 50,000 units in his first year and earning a spot on the Essence Magazine Bestsellers list.

Since Entangled, Elliott has published five titles of his own and two more on behalf of authors signed to Urban Lifestyle Press. For one book, The Ski Mask Way, Elliott was selected to co-author with hip-hop superstar 50 Cent. Along the way, he has continued to look for innovative ways to push his books to his fans while keeping down his overhead.

Elliott is passionate about sharing what he has learned with aspiring authors, and has conducted learning webinars filled with information on what works best for him. He is the author of numerous best-sellers including Dilemma, Street Fame, Treasure Hunter, Dear Summer, Entangled, The Godsend Series and the hugely intriguing Kingpin Wifeys Series.

CPSIA information can be obtained
at www.ICGtesting.com
Printed in the USA
LVHW081724251019
635357LV00013B/599/P